Angels

Samyaza

To Martha, Enjoy! xxooxx P.T. Macias

It's Time, Live On The Dark Side

The Watchers

Angels Of The Fallen
Samyaza

P.T. Macias

Angels Of The Fallen: Samyaza, It's Time, Live On The Dark Side The Watchers By P.T. Macias

Smashwords Edition

Copyright 2015 P.T. Macias

Copyright © 2015 By P. T. Macias.

ISBN-13:978-1519727206

ISBN-10:1519727208

All rights reserved. No part of this book may be reproduced or transmitted in any form or by any means, electronic or mechanical, including photocopying, recording, or by any information storage and retrieval system, without permission in writing from the copyright owner.

This is a work of fiction. Names, characters, places and incidents either are the product of the author's imagination or are used fictitiously, and any resemblance to any actual persons, living or dead, mythology and folklore, events, or locales is entirely coincidental.

This book was printed in the United States of America.

Dedication

I'm dedicating this book with all of love to my husband, children, grandchildren, and family. Thank you for your patience, love, support and believing. Thank you for your love Arturo. Special thanks to my son Andres, daughter Erica, and son Ricardo for their assistance. Te amo!

Special Acknowledgements

I want to give special thanks to Marsha Thomas Berg my assistant and editor. Her dedication to me and my work is amazing and immensely appreciated. Marsha strives to perfect my work.

The Watchers

The Watchers, who are the sons of God, are a superior order of Angels on the highest level of heaven and similar to humans in their appearance.

The fallen Angels have desired the daughters of men and elected to take them as their wives. Several Watchers lead the Angels to mate with women.

The Angels opt to ignore God's decree. They rebel against his ruling and instruct the human race in forbidden lessons.

Their actions initiate disastrous ramifications for both themselves and humanity. Leagues of Angels are chained and imprisoned in eternal penance.

Synopsis

The pure exhaustion of eternal punishment as a fallen has left our sexy but naughty angel, Samyaza, desperate for companionship…desperate to be set free and only you hold the key.

What would you give for one night of unbridled passion? Samyaza gave his life, his freedom ……….everything. After thousands of years of pain and punishment the fallen one thought he'd seen it all…not even close.

Now evil threatens the world and the Watchers are our only hope. Falling from grace was easy, eternal suffering has become common place, wishing for death an everyday occurrence but when faced with a chance for redemption Samyaza fears he could fail.

His test for heavenly grace comes in the form of a beautiful, confident, modern woman who captures the fallen one heart and soul.

Strength he has. Faith in the God that sentenced him to a life in chains he holds close but all may be lost with just one look from this very special woman.

With his life, his soul and his heart on the line, can Samyaza save the world or destroy it?

The Watchers are waiting, wanting…needing you. It's time to live life on the dark side.

Time is running out. Evil forces threaten the very survival of the human race. Our only hope…The Watchers.

The fate of humanity lies in the hands of these twelve stunningly sexy, sinful fallen angels.

Only destiny knows if they will save us or doom to hell.

Table Of Contents

Prologue

One

Two

Three

Four

Five

Six

Seven

Eight

Nine
P.T. Macias
P.T. Macias Series
P.T. Macias Links

Prologue

First Millennium

Samyaza kneels next to the bed with a fixed, fretful expression. He holds onto Beatriz's small, rough hand. His beautiful violet eyes are wide, his face is taut, and his heart races with fear.

He rubs her hard stomach and feels the labor contraction.

Beatriz closes her eyes tight and yells out in pain. Her hair is soaked from the sweat and her lips are dry. Her forehead shines with the fine layer of perspiration.

"Ohoooo……my mighty God, please take this pain away!"

Samyaza leans in closer to her and kisses her sweaty temple.

"My love, everything will be ok. I know that you and our babe will be ok."

He moves his hand to caress her soft pale cheek. He looks over at the midwife.

"Good woman, help my wife and my babe! She's been in labor for two days!"

The midwife ignores him and continues to turn the babe.

"I'm trying my lord, but the babe is stuck. I can't turn him. The babe is breeched."

Samyaza rises from the floor and walks over to the midwife.

"What does that mean? Do whatever you need to do to save my wife and the babe!"

He glares at her frustrated, scared, and anxious. He turns to walk back to Beatriz's bedside.

"My love, everything will be ok."

He kneels down next to her and holds her little hand in his. He watches her closely, then frowns. He glances over at the midwife to access her progress.

The midwife works frantically to turn the babe to the head-down birthing position. She's sweating and her lips are compressed tight, wrinkling around the edges.

Beatriz's beautiful eyes close. Her breathing slows down, and her hand goes limp.

"My love, don't give up!" Samyaza yells, his face pale and scared. He leans down to listen to her heartbeat. He closes his eyes tight.

"Beatriz, don't give up! Don't leave me!"

He turns to look at the midwife stop and step back. Her hands and white apron are soaked with blood and her hands shake.

"My lord. The babe is stuck in the birth canal and I can't stop the bleeding. She's dead." She wrings her hands and looks at Samyaza, shaking and petrified.

"No!"

Samyaza falls onto his knees. He reaches for Beatriz and pulls her into his arms. He buries his face in her neck.

He cries excruciating, deep, long sobs. He holds her tight as his body shakes from the flood of emotions running through his body.

"Beatriz, don't leave me!"

Even thousands of years later, each night is as long and repetitious as each of the past agonizing nights. The dark malevolent demons work to torture and annihilate the souls of the earth's saviors, the angels, the most important guests in hell.

The sinister citadel's underground tunnels are cloaked in swirls of steam and smoke. A perpetual blaze burns in the pits of hell.

The black limestone glows with each flicker of the candlelight. The elaborate silver sconces are mounted to the limestone walls while black candles sit, burning eternally. The flames flicker in a constant dance, creating shadows along the dark hallway that leads to the entrance to the dark tunnel.

The eerie, soul-wrenching screams of the demons echo down the hallway in the second station of hell. The second station is the demon's abode. It also imprisons and punishes the demons that have deliberately disobeyed the laws of Lucifer or Apollyon.

Samyaza, a fallen angel, is desperate and ready to beg for help. He closes his dark violet eyes to concentrate on breathing to gather strength to yell for help.

"Apollyon! I'm ready to seal the pact! Lucifer is not willing to hear my plea!"

He's being punished for leading the fallen angels to sin. He was sent to Lucifer for eternal punishment. Lucifer has eternal control over him.

Samyaza stands in the center of the room naked, dirty, and covered in his own blood which has dried and caked on his body from centuries of punishment.

Thick silver cuffs are clasped to his wrists and ankles, immobilizing him. His fingers and toes are encased in metal gloves forcing them apart in agonizing torture. His long, dirty, black hair hangs over his shoulders, soaked with his crimson blood. His hair reaches his waist in a tangled nest of knots.

Chains are fastened to the cuffs to anchor him to the black limestone floor and ceiling.

He roars in pain, excruciatingly deep cries, with every lash inflicted by the station guard.

The tall muscular demon guard stands behind him, flexing his huge biceps as he swings his strong arm over his shoulder and snaps his wrist in a smooth fluid motion. The black cat o' nine tails' braided leather has nine thick thirty inch tails. Each tail has a silver hook attached, creating the look and feel of barbed wire.

The whip zooms forward and lands on the smooth golden skin. The evil whip inflicts new lacerations, cutting deeply, and mutilating the smooth golden flesh. Streams of dark red blood track down his back, slowly down his firm ass, and flows down his long muscular legs to pool around his feet.

Samyaza's body heals immediately, and the flogging is non-stop.

Apollyon stops in the center of his throne room. He walks over to his sphere to look at Samyaza.

"Fucking hell! Samyaza is one fucking stubborn angel! That's why he's a fallen angel, by choice, not like me by mandate from the heavens."

I'm so fucking tired of hearing his pleas. I'm going to stop this now. Damn it, he deserves this eternal punishment. He allowed his lust for mortal women to consume him and he formed a group of fallen angels to fornicate with human women. The result of their actions was that they begot giant offspring. God's wrath showed no mercy and he is being punished him for eternity.

Apollyon teleports into Lucifer's realm, Hell. He takes long strides, placing one leather shrouded foot in front of the other, and the heels tap on the black limestone floor as he walks. He rapidly approaches the end of the hall and turns to the right to walk down another hall to reach the stairway down to the second station penal chambers.

His huge hands fist at his side, and he clenches his jaw angrily. His lips compress tightly into a straight line, causing his lips turn white from pressure. His swirling, gray-blue eyes glow. His long black shiny hair is tied in a ponytail with a black leather strip.

He urgently takes long strides to reach the last chamber. He raises his right hand and flicks his hand at the guard. He walks into the chamber, squinting his eyes, then glances around the nasty room. He turns to look at the weak, dirty, and pale demon in the center of the room.

"Samyaza, what in the hell do you want? You've been summoning me for the last century! You know damn well that Lucifer is the one you should be talking too! This is his domain, not mine!" Apollyon yells at him through clenched teeth.

Apollyon raises his right arm and snaps his fingers to stop the demon guard from inflicting another lash on Samyaza's back. The demon guard stops, crosses his huge arms, and stands tall, staring ahead, emotionless. He doesn't want to look at Apollyon's swirling gray-blue eyes.

Samyaza blinks rapidly to clear his vision from the pain and to enjoy the temporary respite. He nods at Apollyon and slowly grins.

"Hell Apollyon, I'm glad that you've finally found some mercy, and honor me with your presence. Please, I'm asking for you to help me get out of here. I'm willing to do anything to pay you back.

You're the fallen angel and the powerful Destroyer. I know that you can release me from my eternal punishment. I've paid for my sins and they were only fun sexy sins. For God's sake help me, I implore you!"

Apollyon stands tall. He stretches himself to his full seven feet. His beautiful face contracts into a deep, furious frown. The birthmark on his chest, an intricate woven pattern, flashes brightly from the intense emotions running through his body. He's wearing a leather vest, snug leather pants, and leather boots. He clenches his hands and grinds his teeth.

His swirling gray-blue eyes glare at Samyaza, his nostrils flare, and he emits his florescent black red smoke.

"Fucking hell, Samyaza! I'm not going to release you! You're not my problem. Besides, where would you go? I can't allow you to return to the earth realm to cause chaos. It's a different world and you wouldn't be able to hide with the new technology that the humans have invented."

He turns and paces around the small room, wrinkling his nostrils from the stench. "Hell, you need to bathe!"

"Yeah, tell me about it! I've been here for an eternity and my body is simply done." He lifts his head up to look at Apollyon pace. He closes his eyes, exhausted from the effort.

"I'll have Lucifer visit you and maybe he'll listen to your plea."

He stops in front at Samyaza and nods. He turns to look at the demon guard and smiles down at Samyaza.

"I see that you're being taken care of by my demon. Well, I don't have any reason to release you. By the way, it would give me nothing but issues with Lucifer." He turns around to walk out of the chamber.

"Apollyon! Wait! I have a lot of gold hidden away on the earth realm. I'll give that to you!" Samyaza raises his head to look at him. His head immediately drops from the strain.

Apollyon stops, and then he turns around to glare at him. "Samyaza, I don't need gold or anything else! Remember that I'm the Destroyer and I have everything that I need!"

"I have knowledge of where Asmodeus was sent for his punishment. He was chained by Raphael in utter darkness until judgement day. He's still alive."

Apollyon raises his eyebrow and nods. *Hell yes, now I know where to locate that bastard. Fucking dude wanted to take my station in the heavenly realm. Yes, I'm going to help Samyaza.*

"I'll return soon, after I give this some thought." Apollyon turns and walks out of the chamber.

I can't believe that my faithful angel is going to release Samyaza. I can't allow him to do so. He is my creation, the destroyer. It's not time for him to do my bidding. What is he thinking? I can't allow this!

He opens his clear crystal eyes and turns to look at his guardian angels surrounding his throne. He looks directly at the Archangel Raphael and nods.

"I'm sending you, Raphael, with the power to bind Apollyon's powers and recollections of heaven and hell until it is time for him to execute my orders!"

The angel Raphael appears in the dark tunnel in hell. He walks over to Apollyon as he walks into the hall way and stands next to him, placing his hand on Apollyon's arm.

"Apollyon!"

Apollyon turns to look at him, smiles and nods. "Raphael, it's been an eternity! I'm thrilled to see you."

Raphael nods, he narrows his eyes. "I'm here to honor God's command. He's very displeased with you. I'm binding your powers and recollections until it's time for you to execute his command!"

"What?" Apollyon pulls his arm away and glares at Raphael.

Raphael clasps his hands and together forming an orb which he throws at Apollyon. The glowing blue orb cloaks Apollyon in a restraining capsule.

"Apollyon, I bind your powers and recollections until God has need of you. You will live in the world with minimal power to shield you from evil."

One

Present Millennium

Thousands of years later the night is long and the same continuous torment is inflicted on Samyaza. Unable to withstand the pain, Samyaza yells out again for the millionth time. His soft golden skin is raptured and the dark red blood spurts out, running down his muscular back and his perfectly sculpted round ass, pooling at his feet. The dark stone floor is saturated with his dried blood and the room is cold, yet humid.

In the corner of the room stand four evil demons, enjoying the flogging and yelling with delight. They lean against the cold black limestone. Their skin is grayish-black, wrinkled, and veiny. Their lips are thin and a deep green color.

Their dark black eyes sparkle and their thin lips turn up into a grotesque smiles. Their foul rotten teeth look like a double lines of jagged pointed barbs.

"One more time, Rasp!"

The tall, dark, gray demon calls out in a grating voice as he claps his two claws together. His dark black eyes roll back into his head gleefully.

"Fucking hell!!"

Samyaza yells out, ignoring the demons. His body trembles from the momentary, excruciating pain. Then his body rapidly heals.

The station guard continues the flogging, keeping a steady rhythm, not halting for even a moment.

"Lucifer!!"

Samyaza yells out and faints from the pain. His body has sustained the quick pace, healing instantly, during the last thousands of years but this time it stops. This time his body doesn't regenerate.

This time the injuries continue to bleed. Samyaza's body is in overload. His body shuts down.

Beatriz's shimmering aura appears next to Samyaza. Her long golden-blond hair flows around her shoulders. The white gown drapes on the ground into the pool of red blood.

Beatriz's tears run down her smooth rose-colored cheeks. Her beautiful cornflower-blue eyes look anxiously over Samyaza's body. She strokes his damaged skin, running her fingers down his back.

Yaza, my beloved. Don't give up on life. I'm here near you at all times. I love you and will always love you.

Samyaza opens his violet eyes and he smiles at her.

"Beatriz, my beautiful wife. I miss you so. I want to expire. I want to leave my immortal body and be with you. I wish that I had died when you left me when you were giving birth to our babe."

Beatriz moves her hand up to caress his cheek. She leans in and kisses his dry lips. She smiles through her tears.

Yaza, I miss you and I love you so. You will live and you will love again.

Samyaza eyes close tight. *I still love her so much. This is pure heaven feeling her touch.*

He opens his eyes to look at her but she's not there. His beautiful violet eyes fill with tears.

Lucifer stops pacing and places his hands on his hips when he hears Samyaza calling him.

What the fuck!

He closes his eyes to focus on Samyaza. He sees Samyaza pass out.

The station guard blinks and stops in midair. He shrugs and flogs him again. Samyaza's skin hasn't healed.

Lucifer flashes into the chamber and snaps his fingers. He looks over at Samyaza and then at the station guard.

The station guard immediately stops and stands tall. He looks straight ahead and crosses his arms.

The demons in the corner gather close together and whisper. They glance quickly over to their master, Lucifer.

"We need to wait until he recovers. His body isn't regenerating. Get some water and throw it on him. Maybe he'll wake up and the body will heal."

"Yes, my sire."

The station guard walks over to the wall and grabs the pail full of water. The water is icy cold. The station guard throws it on Samyaza's face.

Lucifer stands tall with his right hand on his silver sword. His bicep flexes as he moves, and he stands straight with his feet spread wide. The silver sword is heavily embellished with precious jewels. He's wearing bracers on his forearms. The silver bracers are engraved with an intricate pattern.

He's a beautiful man with dark black hair. His beard is trimmed to enhance his square jawline. His nose is straight and he has sexy, full, sensual red lips. His beautiful crystal blue eyes glow with his inner power, shining bright.

The black expensive slacks fit him perfectly snug. He looks sexy, dangerous, and beautiful.

Lucifer narrows his eyes and raises his eyebrow.

"Samyaza!"

Samyaza opens his violet eyes slowly and looks over at Lucifer. He's weak and his head falls down onto his chest.

"Lucifer, I beg you to release me. I've paid for my sins. You were released after your penance. I'm done."

His body is beginning to regenerate but not at the usual fast speed.

Lucifer smiles and walks over to the other side of the room. He glares at the demons. Raising his arm, he flips his hand and the demons instantly disappear.

He stops and looks over at the station guard and nods. The station guard disappears.

Lucifer laughs out load at Samyaza. "You're a complete fool! Yeah, I paid for my imprudence."

Samyaza inhales deeply and then opens his eyes. "I've paid for my sins and I don't see why I can't be released! My immortal body is tired and it is done!"

Lucifer grins and walks over to the other side, shaking his head.

"Yeah, but you and your Watchers were consumed with lust! You know that you were sent to me for eternal punishment!"

Samyaza inhales deeply and shudders from the excruciating pain his body feels from the effort.

"Lucifer, we all fell in love with women! The Watchers swore an oath! The oath to not abandon our plans and to bind ourselves in mutual defiance. Tell me what happened to them!"

Lucifer walks over to him and stands in front of Samyaza. He shrugs his shoulders and nods. Turning around, he walks over to the other side of the room He places one hand on the cold black limestone. He then crosses his feet in a very deceptive relaxed pose.

"Samyaza, your clique of fallen angels are also in my realm and in my hands. I can't release you. Archangels Raphael and Uriel imprisoned you and the others."

Lucifer pushes off the wall and walks back to stand in front of him.

Samyaza raises his head slowly to glare at him.

"Yeah, right!"

"Hmmm…you're very angry. Oh, why are you angry at me? I'm not the one that chained you up. You're in my domain but I can't release you!"

He turns on his heels and walks away from Samyaza. Then he suddenly turns to smile a small wicked smile.

"I suggest that you stop calling me!"

Lucifer chuckles and snaps his fingers. The station guard appears and starts the flogging.

The moon is bright and the ocean waves crash against the sand in a fast sensual dance. Crystal walks down the wet sand, looking out into the deep, dark ocean. She looks up into the dark navy sky, her eyes shining brightly, and she sees the shooting star race through the sky.

"I wonder if I wish upon that shooting star, if my wish would be granted."

She stops, rests her hands on her hips, and lets the waves sweep over her bare feet. She squeezes her toes tight and her soft skin breaks out with goosebumps. The cool water sends a chill up her spine.

She smiles a small smile, her dark pink lips turn up at the corners, and her soft rose cheeks appear to flush. Closing her eyes, her long black eyelashes fan across the top of her cheeks. She releases a small sigh.

She breathes deeply, her full breasts rise and fall. The ocean breeze swirls around her long wavy black hair and whips her hair around her shoulders.

I wish, I wish upon the falling star, I wish to have someone to love and be loved.

She smiles a dreamy smile and opens her eyes wide. She raises her dark black eyebrows. She then frowns and sadly pouts her lips.

"Yeah, right! I don't have time to meet anyone with the long days at work. Ah, but I do love my job."

She raises her hands up and gathers her long hair in her hands.

Her breasts rise and fall with each breath. Her nipples pebble and swell under her soft silky top. They look full and creamy, like pearls straining over the top of the silky material.

Her small shorts fit snugly over firm round ass. Her long legs look beautiful and toned as she moves her feet to sink her toes into the wet sand.

"Hell, it's late, and no one is around. I should go home."

She turns to retrace her steps and walks slowly towards her car. She smiles, her even white teeth gleam, and her cute dimples flash.

Her cell phone beeps and she looks at the text from her partner, Bo.

"Hey, Crystal, we have to go in. It's a busy night."

She quickly texts him back. "I'm there in a few."

She runs down the beach and reaches her silver Honda. She opens the car door and slides inside without noticing the tall man standing in the shadows.

She turns the key, turning on her silver Honda, and drives down the road parallel to the coast.

Sorath, the Dark Prince, takes out a black Djarum Black cigarette and flicks his finger. The flame appears and he lights up the cigarette. He leans against the tree and smiles.

He inhales deeply, enjoying the dark spicy cinnamon flavor of the Djarum Black. He slowly exhales, and the smoke swirls around him. His ice blue eyes shine in the dark and he slowly smiles, rocking back onto his heels.

She's perfect for the next virgin sacrifice. I smell her innocence and pure soul. I've seen her visit this beach several times this year. I can smell her when she's here. I can't resist watching her. This is brutal. I can feel the thirst deep in my loins, deep under my skin, and in my blood. The frantic need to possess her soul. I know that I'm going to consume her when I induct her into my sect. She's going to be my disciple, soon, very soon.

He turns abruptly and walks away into the mountainside hidden stairway. The stairway spirals up onto his home back garden that overlooks the Pacific Ocean.

He walks into his huge gardens and looks out into the ocean, nodding at his thoughts.

"I love this view and I feel the pulsations of the souls from deep in the pit. I can't wait to seize it and make it my empire."

Heavy footsteps approach him and he turns around to glare at his servant.

"What is it?"

Sorath stands straight and tall. His broad shoulders stiffen, his lips snarl, and his eyes glow brightly. He flicks his cigarette from his fingers and the butt lands on the soft green grass. He slides his right hand into his black wool slacks. His crisp black shirt sleeves are rolled up his forearms. He pulls out another cigarette, closing his eyelids half way as he lights the next one.

Senator William Jackson walks up the front steps, turning to look around the front yard, then throws his head back to look up to the second story of the Tudor house's façade. The façade is the epitome of darkness and evil. He squints his green eyes and clenches his jaw in disdain.

This place feels so sinister and yet it looks so normal. I feel it. Hell, I don't understand why the caucus wants to nominate this bastard. I don't get it. I don't like him. I don't trust him and I don't believe in him. He has a dark evil aura. I feel it. He's an evil man. I can't locate any background on him. The only background that comes up is that he was adopted by the Santanel family. I can't allow Sorath Santanel to become President. I've heard him state several times that he's the Dark Prince. Damn it. That truly sounds ominous. It sounds like he wants to dominate the world.

He stops at the huge dark wooden doors and rings the huge gargoyle bell.

William turns around to look behind him uneasily. He clenches his fists and grinds his molars. He turns around as the front door opens.

"Hi, I'm Senator Jackson. I'm here for the dinner party."

The butler opens the door and nods.

"Please come in, Senator Jackson."

He steps back, opening the door wide for the Senator.

William follows him down the hallway. His eyes roam all over, and he scrutinizes every detail in the hall. The huge hallway is full of family portraits and a couple of chairs with a side table are placed along the wall. The dark wooden floor glows and shines almost like a mirror.

Senator Jackson walks down the hall, looking at the family portraits.

The Butler stops at the end of the long dark hallway and opens the door at the very end. He holds the door open for him.

"Please enter."

Senator Jackson nods and takes a step inside the study. He looks at the members of the Golden State Democratic Caucus.

He stops at the door and steps aside. He waits for the Butler to close the door.

He then turns to glare at the Senators.

"What the fuck is going on? What are you all doing here?"

Senator Barnes leans back into the black leather chair and raises his hand to inhale deeply of the cigar he's holding. He exhales and shrugs. The smoke swirls around him.

"Calm down, Jackson. He's a good man."

Senator Gino Lombardi smirks. He eyes William as he takes a drink of the Crown Royal in his crystal glass. He licks the drop of brandy from his full lower lip, squints his golden-brown eyes, and then he raises his chin slightly up at an arrogant angle. He shrugs, then abruptly turns away. He's not a very tall man but he's solidly built. His black hair is thinning at the top so he keeps it short to hide it. The dark navy suit fits a little snug around the shoulders and strains at the seams when he shrugs.

"Senator Jackson, you should hear what Senator Santanel is about. You'll be amazed at his charisma, determination, and plans." Gino says loudly, walking towards the empty chair in the large office. He's rough around the edges, having grown up in the poor side of Irvine.

William glares at him and turns to look at the other Senators in the room.

Senator Robert Jones sits relaxed in the black leather chair with his legs crossed. He's tall, thin, and toned with dark, black eyes. His hair is black with silver-gray at the temples. He swirls his crystal glass of whiskey, watching the golden liquid and then suddenly nods at William. He gazes into William's eyes, grinning as if at some secret.

"Santanel only needs one more vote from the caucus for the Presidential nomination. Your vote would make it the majority of the Golden State Democratic Caucus members that would be supporting him. That's why the other Senators aren't here. We believe that you're the man to make this happen. Santanel needs our support and experience. The fact that we're all in our late thirties, early forties makes it easier to assimilate into his agenda. The majority of us are single and that helps. He'll take care of us."

"I don't see what he has to offer to the United States or us. I believe that Senator Edward Morgan would do an amazing job. We were planning on supporting the Washington Caucus in nominating him. Why the change of heart?"

Senator Max Slimestone jumps up from the chair and walks over to Jackson, sneering at him. He takes out a cigarette and lights it up, looking at William. He inhales deeply and exhales the dark gray smoke around them.

"William, trust us. You'll learn to love the guy! He's an amazing man and I totally support his agenda. I know that you'll understand after you hear him out. He needs us to support him, and to protect his interests."

"What the fuck!"

William turns to glare at the other Senators in the room, who are drinking and smoking. He strides quickly across the room, his suit jacket flaps open, and his black leather shoes sink deep into the expensive carpet. He wants to talk to Senator Edward Miles. He stands in front of Senator Miles with his hands on this waist.

"Edward, tell me that you're not insane. Tell me that I'm not the only one that sees that Santanel is not what he appears."

Edward looks up at him and shrugs his wide shoulders. He turns to look over at the other Senators and then glares at William. He pushes up from the chair and slaps William on the back.

"William, you're overreacting and overthinking this. It's not a big deal because we could always nominate Senator Morgan for the next elections.

Santanel is the right man. He's perfect and we need to support him."

Senator Lewis Lancaster and Senator Martin Drone stand and walk over to William, smiling.

"William, it's all good." Senator Lancaster punches his arm.

William clenches his jaw tight, his muscles flex and he outright asks him. *Hell, I don't care if this is insensitive on my part, but what the fuck! I need to know because more than half the caucus is in agreement of this absurd nomination.*

"Since when are you two single? You're happily married for years."

"Yeah, I was, but Janet took off with some jerk!" Senator Lancaster growls. He takes a long, deep drink of his whiskey.

William winces, surprised. "Sorry to hear that, Lewis."

Damn it! I need a drink.

Senator Jackson walks over to the window to look out. He leans over to the small table to grab a crystal glass, then grabs the crystal decanter, and pours the golden whiskey into the glass.

Senator Jackson turns to look out of the window narrowing his eyes as he sees Sorath in the gardens. He narrows his eyes to focus on his face. He watches Sorath walk up the stairs and onto the patio.

Hell, I'll be damn if I'll support his pompous ass. I don't see what the others see in him. I'm not going to support him.

He raises his arm to bring the crystal glass to his lips. He takes a drink of the gold whiskey, pursing his lips. He closes his eyes to enjoy the burn running down his throat.

"Master Sorath, the chamber is ready."

"Excellent. Have my guests arrived?"

"Yes, my lord. They're waiting for you in the office.

Sorath smiles and turns to walk towards his huge home. He walks up the rocky steps and into his patio. He then walks towards the French doors that lead into his office.

He smiles at the group of men sitting around in the black leather armchairs, smoking his cigars and drinking his liquor.

"Evening, Senators. It's a pleasure to have you in my home."

He turns to smile at them as he stops at the door of the office. He waves his hand to take control of the Senator's minds.

He pushes the black heavy wood door closed. He turns to look over at Senator Jackson, standing at the window looking out into the ocean.

"I'm pleased to see that you made it here on time, Senator Jackson. I would like to get your commitment because you're the only vote that I need to get on the election ballot. I know that you know it's time. It's been a long time coming and I'm anxious to govern the United States. I'm ready now for this and it's time for me to take my place in the world. I need to be the President of the United States."

He walks over to William and slaps him on the back gazing into his green eyes. Sorath's ice blue eyes glow and the energy travels into William's green eyes, manipulating his mind."

William eyes widen and his mind hears his thoughts.

I can hear him! He's communicating with my mind. Fuck! I'm paralyzed. I can't move my body, and I can only breathe. What's happening to me?

You will back me because I'm the Dark Prince and this is the beginning of my dominion. You

will be my guardian, William. You will be my servant. You are my disciple, and you will obey my every command.

Crystal opens her car door and runs into her small apartment. She opens the door and turns on the lights. She looks around the small living room. She closes her door and locks it as she continues to monitor the room.

I hate the feeling of being watched. I can't shake it off and I always feel it when I'm at the beach. I must be crazy.

Crystal takes long strides down the hallway, her leg muscles flex, and her full breasts bounce up and down. The sexy silky top rises up to her rib cage as she pulls it off. Her black lacey demi bra looks beautiful showcasing her creamy breasts. She looks into the mirror and stops. She turns to the right and to the left.

"Hell, I'm losing a lot of weight and I don't know why."

She pulls down her white shorts and looks at herself in her small bikini.

"Good, I look good. Ok, well I don't have to worry about my body, geeze. I'm going to have to go out on some date soon. I'm tired of being lonely."

She walks into the shower and takes off her bra and bikini underwear. She turns on the shower water, steps inside, and proceeds to take a cold shower.

"Yeah, this really woke me up."

Crystal runs the soapy cloth over her firm body. She leans down to remove the sand from her feet. She quickly rinses off. She turns off the shower and pulls the towel from the wall hanger.

She walks out of the shower and pats dry her soft, glowing rosy skin. She frowns and puckers her lips.

I need to hurry. I wish that we weren't called in. I really wanted to relax. Hmmm, I wouldn't be bored at work. Time always flies.

She pulls on her clean bikini underwear and then a matching clean bra.

She turns around and pulls her hair into a ponytail and grabs her lipstick.

Apollyon walks down the huge hallway in the laboratory in the research station located beside the warm Southern California coast.

He moves his head to the right and left.

Hell yeah, I'm alone. All the scientists went to sleep.

He holds onto his water bottle with his left hand and he then pushes the thick eyeglasses up his straight nose.

He wears the eyeglass to hide his swirling gray-blue eyes from the humans. He walks over to his desk to enter the new research data. He slides onto his black chair and starts to enter the results.

Yeah, this is a great breakthrough. I'm thankful that I can work on this team. It keeps me from going crazy. My time here is almost up and what then? I'm getting tired of being in this limbo. I can't use my powers or talk to any of the Angels. Geeze, not even Lucifer.

I sure as hell can't talk to the Archangels or God. Damn it, how long is this going to take? I've been working different human jobs for thousands of years.

I'm glad that recently the jobs have been more challenging and interesting. Oh hell, I really miss my palace and my bed.

I know that Lucifer is taking care of my legions but hell.

He closes his eyes and rubs his forehead. He then leans back onto the chair, reading the data.

Ok, that's all I have. I'm going to bed. Not because I'm exhausted but because I'm feeling frustrated. I need to sleep this off.

He pushes off the chair. His long strong legs flex, and he stands stretching out his long arms above him. The chair rolls away and crashes into the desk on the other side. He turns to his right to look over at the door.

Jill smiles a small shy smile at him. She crosses her arms below her breasts and blushes.

"I'm sorry to creep up on you, Lyon, but I thought that I would be alone. I really wanted to start the new phase of the testing." She raises her shaking hand up to her hair to push back her bangs.

Apollyon has the humans call him Lyon but it is pronounced Leon. He nods at her and shrugs his huge shoulders.

"Hey Jill, I'm heading to bed now. No worries." He walks up to her.

"I have entered the last test results. That might help you with the next phase."

Jill nods her head several times. She blushes, having Lyon so close to her.

"Good, that's good. Thanks."

She walks away nervously from him towards her desk.

Lyon shrugs and walks off down the hall towards his small room. He takes long strides, the heel of his leather boots tap on the white tile, the sound echoing through the hallway. He takes of his eyeglasses and shoves them into his white lab coat pocket.

Apollyon opens the door to his room, he steps inside, and he looks around. He then closes the white door. He locks it and then takes of his long white lab coat. He hangs it on the chrome coat hanger on the door.

He pulls up his black t-shirt, his biceps flexing and bulging as he pulls it up over his head. His beautiful hair comes loose from the leather strip.

Lyon unbuttons his leather pants and pulls them down. His engorged cock pops forward. He sits on his bed and unlaces his boots. He pulls off the black leather boots and places them on the side of his bed.

He looks down at his long, aching cock. He takes his cock into his hands. His right hand runs up and down in a slow sensual strokes. He stops at the base and cups his tight balls. He moves his hand up to stroke from the base up to his sensitive deep purple crown. He closes his eyes, his full lips open slightly, and he groans.

"I need relief and I don't want to touch any of my associates. I know that Jill wants me and she wouldn't turn me away, but I don't want to complicate the working environment. I know that it would make nothing but problems."

His body tenses and then he exhales, releasing a heavy stream onto his bed. His black-red florescent smoke cloaks him.

He falls back onto his back on the bed. He closes his beautiful swirling gray-blue eyes.

Hell, I really need to move on. The little power that I have is worthless, it's a joke. I have to sleep often to generate power. I can't truly do much. I need to find a way to regain my powers. I have to locate a way to enter hell to get to my realm.

He falls asleep and his body begins to relax in his sleep. He needs to sleep for a couple hours to regain some of his limited power.

The Powers, the Warrior Angels, are known as potentates. They fight evil spirits that seek to wreak chaos through the humans. The Warrior Angels protect the cosmos and humans from evil

The Warrior Angels stand at the outer edge of the heavenly realm, monitoring the humans. They spread their huge, shimmering, black wings.

The Warrior Angel's chief is Samael. He stands tall and his long, golden hair flows around his shoulders. He turns to his right to look over at his brethren. Camael, Raphael, Verchiel are his counterparts and are angels of darkness.

"Samael, thou shall announce that it's time to protect the Citadel and fight the Dark Prince and his Legions." God commands his Warrior Angel.

Warrior Angel Samael appears to Apollyon in his sleep. He spreads his majestically shimmering black wings and leans in close to Lyon's ear. He whispers to him.

"Apollyon, it's time for you to regain your powers to fight the evil that is brewing in the underworld. Your Citadel needs to remain sealed until God mandates that it is time to release his wrath."

"The Dark Prince has come of age. He's gaining power every day and will soon rise. He's gathered his guardians and is now going to induct the demons to his faction."

Apollyon, you must open your eyes, listen to your heart, and follow your instinct. You need to search for your powers and with each action you shall regain your powers. In the process of seeking your powers, you will be forced to make challenging decisions."

Angel Samael disappears as he waves his hand over Apollyon's head.

Two

During the middle of the night Crystal and her partner, Bo Davis, walk out of the emergency room to their red emergency paramedic van.

"Hey, I'm exhausted. I hope that we don't get called in again. I need some rest."

Crystal pulls off her hairband and shakes out her long silky hair. She then pulls the handle on the door and slides onto the passenger seat.

Bo slides into the driver's seat and starts the van. He looks over at her, noticing that she's almost asleep.

"Yeah, Crystal I'm tired too. We'll be at the station in a few."

He turns the steering wheel and turns off the radio. He adjusts his eyeglasses and drives down the road, watching as the homeless scurry into the dark shadows.

"Hey, Crystal I have awesome news. Betty and I are getting married."

Crystal opens her eyes wide and grins. She whistles and sits up in the chair.

"That's really awesome news, Bo. I'm happy that she said yes. You see, you were worried for nothing."

She throws back her head and laughs, closing her eyes.

Bo looks over at her, smiling. He shrugs his huge shoulders and drives the van into the parking space.

"You know that I wasn't sure because you women are funny odd creatures. You say one thing but do another sometimes."

Crystal stops laughing and turns to look at him. She reaches over to slap his right shoulder.

"Well, I told you that she would say yes. Women don't spend two years with a guy if they don't want them."

Bo grins, and nods. "Yes, you were right. I was scared shitless when I asked her. Now I'm scared shitless about the wedding."

"Yeah, you have no reason to be scared. Enjoy the moment, it's special, and you deserve it."

Bo nods, and turns towards her. He stops smiling and grabs his jacket on the floor.

"I'm sure that you'll meet someone soon."

"Yeah, you think so?"

"Yeah, I do."

Crystal smiles and turns around to open the door. She slides out of the van and walks towards the station to change into her street clothes.

Sorath turns to look at the Senators sitting in the black leather chairs in his office. He releases William and walks over to the wall that has the entire wall full of books. He stands tall, his face completely deadpan, and he gazes into each Senator's eyes.

"Senators, my faithful sentinels. We now have the Golden State Caucus as my disciples. Follow me, I'm going to induct Senator Jackson."

Sorath turns slightly to the right side and slides his hand over the decorative scroll on the bookcase. The bookcase slides to the left and stops when it reaches the wall.

A small hallway is exposed and a black wooden door is closed without a handle.

Sorath waves his hand and the door slides open. The dark stairway is revealed. The stairway walls are made of rock and several hanging fire lamps are attached from the ceiling from black chain. The fire dances, casting eerie shadows and a thick layer of smoke down the stairway.

Sorath walks down the stairway, leading his disciples to his throne to perform the initiation ritual.

Senator Jackson, William, follows him down the dark stairway that leads to the basement.

Sorath stops at the base of the stairway and turns to look at his disciples. His blue eyes glow and he leers evilly at them. He transmits to the Senators lined up the stairway.

My disciples, I require you to undress and drape on the black cloak.

Sorath then glances over to William and sneers.

"William, take your clothes off and drape one of the black cloaks around you."

Sorath takes off his black shirt and allows it to drop onto the floor. He then unzips his black slacks, his engorged cock springs forward as he slides off his pants. He looks at William undressing.

He reaches for one of the black cloak that hangs from the peg on the stone wall and pulls it on.

The Senators behind William wait patiently for him to finish.

Sorath turns and walks slowly to his altar. He stops at the base and turns to look at the young women fully naked and standing down each side of the dais.

Several spicy incense cones burn at the altar. The room is satiated with pungent sexy spicy cinnamon incense. The cinnamon is used to inflame the senses, passion and lust to run unbridled in a heady powerful need of desire. It's a strong aphrodisiac to use in the powerful fire energy ritual.

"William, I command thee to go to the table."

William walks slowly towards the table and looks at the Senators walking towards the back to stand in a circle.

Sorath walks over to a tall blond young woman on the right.

"My sweets, you look lovely."

He pulls her into his arms and runs his hands down her back to grasp her firm ass. He slides his hungry tongue into her willing mouth. He devours her mouth and consumes her soul. He then places her onto his alter and spreads her legs.

His fingers rub her swollen flesh and sinks one finger inside her tight pussy. He leans down and sucks her honey coated pussy and slides his hot velvety tongue inside to suck up her honey. He growls against her pussy and rubs his face into her hot flesh.

The young woman quivers and moans.

My Sweets, I love me some young sweet pussy. Truly a treat after a long day.

He pulls away and walks over to the next young woman. He repeats his unbridled actions.

He pulls away from the last girl and he turns around to look at his disciples.

The young girls stand motionless, their nectars running down their legs, and their breasts are swollen. The Senators stand around stroking their hard cocks. Their eyes shine brightly full of lust. They wait for the ritual to begin.

Sorath regards William, who stands in the center of the room next to the table.

William attempts to talk. *What the hell is this? I can't move or talk. The Senators are all under his spell. I can't stop this.*

Sorath is deeply and completely consumed in desire. He shrugs the black cloak off. He walks towards William, each muscle in his tone body flexes with each step. His blue eyes gleam, and his cock weeps.

He stops in front of William and places his hands on his shoulders. He slides off the black cloak, allowing it to fall onto the floor.

He steps back to look at William from the tip of his toes. He stops to behold William's swollen cock. He looks over William's beautiful abdominal muscles, then he raises his eyes to look over his strong chiseled chest, and up to his light brown hair with gold highlights.

"My Pet, you're gorgeous. I can't wait to suck your amazing cock, and fuck your tight ass. You're such a treat."

Sorath, the Dark Prince, moves both of his hands up towards the ceiling to start his chant. He slowly turns in a circle as he chants.

"I cast the circle of forces to create a sacred boundary between our life and the world powerful elements, the meeting place of power, lust, rapture, and wealth. To feel the strength that will rise before the custodian to the north, south, east, and west, and the custodian of earth, air, fire, and water. Help your Dark Prince's cause, in the name of the ruler and rings we cast up the great circle of power!"

"My disciples shall honor me, guard me, and serve my every need. I own all your souls, bodies, and minds. I have your complete devotion!"

The Dark Prince opens his hands and his palms are raised up and then he moves them down as he turns in a circle. The circle of fire erupts around Sorath and William, enclosing them in their own sphere.

William's green eyes are feverish, consumed with red hot desire. He stares at Sorath's engorged cock and his mouth waters.

I want some like I never did before. I need his touch on my sensitive skin.

Sorath's eyes shine brightly, his lust, and his energy cloaks William.

He takes a few steps towards William, his left hand grabs the base of his cock, and his right hand slides up to caress his cock. The crown is shiny, coated with his seed.

"William Jackson, my disciple, I'm consuming your soul, your mind, and your body. You're mine to do with as I please. You will obey my every command, desire, and need. You will protect me with your life. This shall be my bidding, and this shall be your mission."

Sorath reaches out for William and pulls him into his arms, rubbing their cocks together, and they hiss.

Fuck, this is hot!

William looks deep into Sorath's gleaming blue eyes.

The Dark Prince leans in closer and takes William's mouth in a deep fierce kiss.

Sorath slides his hungry tongue inside Williams's mouth, extracting his soul. He rubs his tongue all over every single millimeter of William's mouth.

Oh hell! This is incredibly hot and I'm totally turned on by Santanel!

Sorath pulls back. He gazes into William's passionate eyes. He raises his arm to his lips and bites his vein. Bright red blood spurts out and he moves it to William's mouth.

Drink my pet. Drink my life substance. You're now entirely mine. I'll always know where you are.

William groans as he sucks Sorath's blood. His feverish green eyes gaze into Sorath's blue eyes.

Oh fucking hell, he's so hot! His blood tastes rich and spicy. He's branding me. I'm burning up with red hot lust. I need to fuck him and be fucked. I feel my soul is merging to his.

The Dark Prince pulls his arm away and licks his wounds. He then leans in to take another hungry kiss.

William slides his tongue inside the Dark Prince's mouth, and moves his right hand to touch Sorath's huge swollen hot cock. He clasps his hand around his purple crown and then slides his left hand fingers down to cradle his scorching balls.

That's it, my pet, take hold of my balls.

Sorath transmits to William as he runs his huge hands down his back to grasp his firm ass. He pulls his huge round orbs apart and slides one long finger to rub his tight asshole.

William shudders and pushes his ass back to encourage him.

Sorath pulls back, laughing. He growls, gazing deeply into William's beautiful green eyes.

"Senators and girls, enjoy the ritual!"

He leans down and runs his hot tongue over William's sensitive nipples. He then bites them and sucks each nipple, crazy with passion.

William hisses and trembles.

"Master, your mouth is so scorching hot!"

Sorath releases his nipple and falls down onto his knees. He takes William's throbbing cock in his hands and licks the creamy glistening fluid from his wide red head. He holds onto his firm ass as he sucks William's cock's head, enjoying every second.

He pulls away from the William's cock to lick around the crown. He runs his velvety tongue down his cock, tracing every throbbing vein.

Sorath sucks the wide red head back into his mouth and releases it like a pop.

"Fuck! Oh, yes!"

William yells, throwing back his head, his neck muscles flexing, and his neck vein throbbing. He trembles with fiery rapture.

Sorath releases his hard cock and rubs his cheek along William's cock inhaling, deeply.

Pet, you have the most incredible cock. Simply mouthwateringly scrumptious.

He takes his hand away from William's ass and turns him around towards the table. He spreads his legs and leans in closer to his tight ass.

"My pet, push your virgin ass back!"

William leans over the table and pushes his ass out, trembling. His cock is hard as steel, aching to fuck Sorath.

"Master, please, I can't wait!"

Sorath spreads his ass, he leans in, and places his full red hot lips to Williams's tight delectable asshole. He moves his hands forward to grasp William's huge hard cock.

Oh yes my Pet, you have a delicious tight asshole. Sweet and pure. I love this, I'm the first to taste your charms.

Sorath transmits as he sucks William's tight asshole with his hot lips. He then licks the bundle of nerves and pushes his tongue into the tight muscle as he strokes William's pulsating cock.

I love your huge cock and I can't wait for you to fuck me. I'm enjoying your induction ceremony my Pet.

William growls and pushes his ass back into Sorath's hot tongue.

"Yes Master, I want you to fuck my ass!"

Sorath plunges his tongue inside his tight ass enjoying his taste and smell.

William eyes look frantically around, not seeing, but only feeling the red hot insane need to be fucked.

Fuck, he's driving me insane. I'm on fire, my blood is fiery red.

Sorath grins and stands up. He grabs his hard engorged cock and slides his purple head into the tight muscled ring. He pushes and he pops his wide cock head inside. He penetrates William's tight virgin ass and buries his cock deeply to the hilt, growling.

Pet, such a tight ass! Such a treat! Pet, yes, you have the sweetest asshole ever!

William yells out in total rapture. "Fucking hell! The burn is painfully delicious. I love your cock! Hell yes, fuck me Master!"

Sorath grabs William's cock to stop him from coming as he fucks him fast and deep.

William yells out and whimpers. "Master, faster!"

He pushes his ass back to take Sorath's big cock deeper inside. He straightens up to lean into Sorath's chest to kiss him.

Sorath takes his mouth. He devours William's tongue, and moves his hands down to stroke his engorged cock as he penetrates deeply.

My Pet, I'm coming inside your tight ass.

He moves his mouth to William's neck and bites hard into his soft flesh marking William as his. The intricate mark is seared into William's neck.

Sorath releases into William's tight ass, he yells out his release, and holds William's steel hard cock tight.

William groans, his passion filled eyes wide. Sorath pulls out of his tight ass and turns him around.

Fuck me my Pet, fuck me hard.

Sorath turns around and spreads his legs wide. He pushes his ass out.

William stares at his round firm ass and leans down to take a bite of that firm flesh. *Yes, sweet ass. Why didn't I ever desire some tight man's ass?*

Sorath growls and pushes his ass back.

Come on my Pet, eat my tight hole. I want to feel your hot mouth and tongue.

William trembles. He falls onto his knees, and spreads Sorath's cheeks apart. He stares at the tight puckered flesh, leans in, and sucks Sorath's tight asshole.

He then slides his hot tongue around the tight edge moaning. He sucks the tight flesh and runs his tongue over it.

This ass is sweet, tight and delicious. I want to fuck his tight hole. I'm so hot and hard.

Sorath pushes his ass into his mouth, growling and emitting flames.

Fuck me Pet, fuck me!

William pulls away from his asshole and stares. He pushes his finger around the edge and sinks it inside.

Fuck yes!! That feels so good. I want your big hard cock deep inside my ass. My Pet, fuck me!

William stands and takes his throbbing cock in his hands and pushes it inside Sorath's tight muscle. He pushes harder to slide all the way deep inside Sorath's tight ass.

"Master, most super tight ass ever!"

William starts to pound into Sorath's ass fast, hard, and deep. He holds onto Sorath's hips and jack knifes in a fluid fast speed.

"Fuck yes! I knew that your cock was incredibly delicious!!"

Sorath yells, pushing his ass back to take more of Williams's big cock.

William reaches his release and collapses over Sorath's back. He shudders in deep excruciating rapture.

Master, I loved this. William thinks as he pulls out.

Sorath turns around and pulls William into his arms to kiss him deeply. He seizes his soul, he consumes his body, and brands his mind.

My Pet, we've only just begun our night. I plan on enjoying your luscious cock. I think I love your cock more than my pussy. I'm not sharing you tonight…maybe never. I feel a special bond with you, as if our DNA fused.

William trembles and returns Sorath's kiss with frantic fury and lust. William greedily grabs his hard purple wide cock's head.

The Dark Prince moves his hand down to rub his palm around William's red head. William's cock springs to attention, hard as steel, and ready for more.

The night indeed had only begun, filled with writhing, sweaty bodies and moans of pleasure heard from all in the room. A night full of debauchery.

Apollyon wakes after a couple of hours of sleep. His body has fully charged to the full limited capacity. He opens his beautiful swirling gray-blue eyes, his long lashes fan above his eyebrows.

He pushes up into a sitting position and looks around his room.

"I smell some strange essence. Was someone here?"

He swings his legs over the side of the bed and stands up. His powerful legs muscles flex and his tight abdominal muscles quiver as he pushes up from the bed. His swollen cock throbs and he places his right hand on his head, rubbing the liquid.

Damn, I'm always so damn hot.

He walks over to the bathroom and takes a quick shower.

Moments later, he walks out of the shower and walks over to the closet. He slides the door open and pulls a gray shirt off the hanger and a pair of black leather pants. He drops them on the bed and he takes the pants and pulls them up over his hips. He moves his hands to adjust his cock. He hisses as he touches his sensitive cock. He buttons up the pants and grabs the shirt.

Lyon runs his fingers through his long silky black hair and then takes the leather strip to tie it into a ponytail.

He then takes some socks from the small night stand and pulls them on. He quickly pulls on his leather boots.

"Hell, why am I in a hurry? I'm off today and I don't really have anywhere to go. I can't shake this urgency off. I need to leave this room clean and I'll wipe their memories of me. I'm glad that I have a little power to conceal who I am and to protect myself."

Lyon waves his hand and clears the room of all of his belongings. He takes his jacket from the door peg and walks out of his room. He walks down the hallway and stops. He waves his hand in a circle to sweep the entire building removing his essence, the scientist team's memories of him, and any trace of his presence. He then turns and strides towards the huge steel doors. His long legs move fluidly in perfect synchronization as he sets one foot on the floor, then pushes off with the other foot.

Lyon pushes the doors open and walks out of the research laboratory. He stops at the entrance and looks out towards the ocean. He looks at the twilight right before dawn breaks. He inhales deeply and squints his eyes. He nods his head, looking at the faint light in the horizon.

Yes, this is the time that I feel the connection with my powers, for a small moment, I feel the vibes. The bonds are tough to break, and my powers smolder.

"Yes, I feel that I have to leave. I can't stay here any longer. I need to leave, just like I left the Antarctica research lab. I feel the need to leave. I have to find a way inside Lucifer's domain to get to the Citadel. I'm tired of this. I know that I can't continue in this limbo."

Lyon stands tall, his broad shoulders pushed back in a proud stance, and his chin raised high with purpose. He then walks away, determined to reach his goal.

He walks down the building towards his black Dodge pickup. He opens the door and slides into the seat.

A few moments later, he drives down the coast towards the powerful energy that he feels calling him.

"Apollyon, hear me! I implore you to release me. My body is too drained and I need to rest from this eternal torment."

Samyaza yells as loud as he can. His energy is travelling the distance and vibrating through the world.

"Damn it, I feel the energy calling me but I can't hear who it is or what they want."

This seclusion has been too damn long and I'm done. How long is this going to take? My skin feels alive, I feel the energy of something menacing formidable, and something that I know will change everything. I need to return to my Citadel. I need to talk to Lucifer. I need to visit Samyaza, Azazel, Ramiel, Arakiel, Kabaiel, Armaros, Daniel, Êzêqêêl, Zaqiel, and Baraqiel. They're the leaders of the fallen angels and the ones that are being punished until judgement day.

I know that they're as frustrated as I am with this eternal imprisonment. Yeah, I'm free but my damn powers are bound. I might as well be fucking imprisoned. I know that they must feel this energy that I feel. It's not the same as ours.

He drives down the coast, concentrating on the energy force that's pulling him. He squints and searches the road for any signs. He opens his mind and soul.

The dawn is breaking and William is sleeping in Sorath's bed. He's naked and beautiful.

Sorath's watches him sleep, grinning. He moves his hand down William's abs and stops. He runs his fingers down William's amazing cock. He leans in and sucks wide red head.

Who would had thought that he was going to be so damn delicious? I never thought that I would want a man in my bed for eternity. Damn, his cock drives me wild. I love to suck his cock and to get fucked by him.

He licks around the red crown and sucks the head inside his mouth, taking him deeper into his throat.

Ah yeah, I never really allowed a man to fuck my mouth. Hell, this cock has me perpetually turned on. All I wanted all night was his cock to fuck me, which is insane. I can't allow him to ever learn the power that his cock has over me.

William groans, and shifts his hips, ready to fuck Sorath's mouth.

"Master, I'm going to fuck your mouth!"

My Pet, yes. I want you to fuck my mouth. I want to taste your seed. I want you to come inside my mouth. I can't get enough of your cock.

William pulls his cock out and turns around. He slides his cock back inside Sorath's mouth and takes Sorath's big purple cock in his mouth.

They play and suck the other's cock for a while, enjoying their favorite treat.

A few hours later William walks into his office sore and confused.

What the hell happened? I feel so cheap and dirty. When did I ever want a cock to fuck me? He has control over me and my body. Just thinking of him has me in a raging painful need. His touch and smell drive me insane. I can't stop it and I hate that I love his fucking cock. I can't wait to suck his purple head.

I feel a strong connection with Sorath and I'm not sure if it is him manipulating me. Did our souls truly merge as one? Damn it! I felt our souls merge. Could it be possible that what he said is true? Could it be our DNAs, our chemistry? This is insane.

I'm not sure that I can stay away from him. I know that he wants me at his side all the time. He wants me to move in with him. That's crazy but yet so damn appealing.

His hand trembles as he slides it down his pants to stroke his aching cock. He walks over to the window to look out. He looks towards Sorath's house on the coast.

"Oh hell, I need him!"

He unzips his pants and pulls out his aching engorged cock. He looks down and notices Sorath's mark on his groin.

"When the fuck did he do that? He marked me!"

He fingers his mark and shudders. He looks over at his cell phone and sees the text message from his fiancée.

Hell, I forgot about Carol. Damn it. I never felt the same with Carol when I made love to her. I'm such a whore. How did I allow a man to fuck me all night and I fucked him just as much.

I'm not going to talk to Carol yet because I can't face her. I feel so guilty. I have to think.

Three

Samyaza is resting on hot floor naked and exhausted. His matted, dirty, soaked hair fans around his shoulders.

The tall, thin demon walks into the room to place a tray of food in front of him. He stands in front of Samyaza, waiting for him to respond. He crosses his long skinny arms and glares down at him. His dark gray skin is wrinkled and dry. His green lips are full and he slowly smiles, exposing a double row of pointed sharp teeth.

"Samyaza, here's your meal. You need to hurry because you only have a few moments to eat."

The tall demon's raspy voice echoes in the room.

Samyaza opens one beautiful violet eye and then closes it, groaning.

The demon places his hands on his waist and glares at Samyaza.

"Samyaza!"

Samyaza startles and he slowly opens his beautiful eyes. He pushes himself up into a sitting position. He raises his hands up to push his matted dirty hair from his eyes.

"Fuck!"

"Hurry up!"

The demon leaves the room, slamming the door. The door vibrates on its hinges from the force.

Samyaza looks at his food and takes a small drumstick. He brings it up to his mouth to take a bite.

"I'm so fucking tired of this insane cycle. Punishment, eat, punishment, eat. It's never ending. I only want to cease to exist, yet it's not allowed. Why the fuck not? I'm done."

Samyaza eats the drumstick. He drops the bones on the tray. He takes another drumstick, too tired to cut up the steak. He closes his eyes as he chews the meat.

I wonder what the vibe is. It's an exceedingly strong skin crawling energy but it's not the same as ours. Where is it coming from?

He reaches for the glass of water and takes a few swallows. Then he places the glass on the tray.

"Now I'm starting to feel better. Yeah, the food and the small relief is charging up my body. Hell, the nightmare begins again. I don't get it? Why this extreme punishment when I only wanted a wife and family. I can handle being exiled from the heavens, but this is too much. Really, was that so awful? Now, I want to leave this hell hole, yeah. I want to live my life as a human man, not a fallen angel!"

Lucifer appears in front of Samyaza, grinning, and walks around him. He stops in front of him and laughs.

"Samyaza, you look terrible and smell awful! I think it's time for your bath. It's been a long time since you had one."

Lucifer spreads his long legs and crosses his powerful arms. His beautiful blue eyes gleam, emitting his powerful energy.

"Luc, you're such an ass at times. You're enjoying my suffering and only give me a bath when you want to enjoy my misery at getting drenched in my own blood!"

Lucifer grins, shrugs his huge shoulders, and drops his hands to his side, nodding. He snaps his fingers as he walks away from Samyaza.

"Sam, it's time for your bath and then it's time to start your punishment. I'll return in……….hmmmmmm…..when I please!"

Samyaza glares at him, his beautiful violet eyes shine, and he clenches his jaw. *I'm not going to say a word because he'll take longer to give me a meal.*

The station demon appears and stands at his place.

Lucifer snaps his fingers and the chains and cuffs move to encircle around Samyaza's ankles and wrists. He's pulled up to the flogging position.

"Have you seen Lyon? It's been a long time since he's visited me."

Lucifer shrugs his shoulders and turns away. He looks out into space, searching for Lyon's energy aura. He then shakes his head and turns to look at Samyaza with his right eyebrow lifting.

"Sam, I haven't seen or heard from him in a long time. I can't locate him but I can feel his energy aura. It's really faint."

Samyaza squints his eyes. "You're not messing with me?"

Lucifer looks at him solemnly. "No, I'm not."

Apollyon drives his black Dodge pickup next to the gas tank to fuel up. He pulls out his wallet to extract his debit card. He slides it into the card scanner and pulls it out. He grabs the gas nozzle and inserts it into the fuel tank.

Lyon leans against the cab on his truck and turns to look across the street into the ocean. The waves crash against the rocks, foaming as they crash and retrieve.

A silver BMW pulls up to the other side of the gas tank. Lyon turns to look at the gas meter.

Sorath opens the car door and slides out in a quick fluid motion. He turns to look around and shrugs. *Fuck, no attendants to fuel up. Damn it. Why did they do away from such an awesome service?*

The red and blue lights flash brightly and the sirens blare loudly as the police car approaches the gas station. The police pull up behind Sorath's silver BMW.

The officer opens his door. He slides out of the car, leaving the car running. He places his hands on his black leather belt and he takes a few steps forward. He looks over at Sorath.

Sorath turns to look at the officer. The scowl on his face deepens, and he stands with his left hand on the roof his car and his right hand on his waist.

"Sir, you were speeding and you didn't pull over. I need your driver's license, please."

The officer stops in front of him. He looks Sorath in the eyes.

Sorath smiles, his blue eyes gleam, and he gazes into the officer's brown eyes.

"Officer, you didn't read my license plate? You would have learned that I'm Senator Sorath Santanel. Your job is not to stop me, especially for a ticket. What's your badge number?"

Officer Ford's eyes narrow. He shakes his head, and shrugs.

"Senator Santanel, that doesn't mean that you're immune to speeding tickets. Sir, I have requested that you hand over your driver's license."

Sorath takes a step forward, he stops grinning at Officer Ford. He stands in front of Officer Ford only a few inches away from him. His blue eyes gleam brighter as he gazes into the officer's brown eyes.

"Officer, you're going to return to your car and you're going to forget all about me. You will worship and protect me at all times."

Sorath opens his mouth slightly and leans a little closer to him. He extracts his soul as he continues to hold his gaze.

You're my disciple and my guardian. You will obey my every command and desire.

He stops gazing into the officer's wide eyes and steps back. He leans against his car, smiling at the officer.

"It's a pleasure meeting you, Officer Ford. I'm in a hurry. We will talk later."

Officer Ford smiles and nods. He looks over at Lyon and then at the station store.

"Yes, Sir."

He turns around and walks to his car. He opens the door and slides inside the seat. He shifts gears and pulls back out onto the street. He waves at Sorath and drives away.

Sorath grabs the gas nozzle from the tank and inserts it into his car. He stands next to his car, looking into the ocean. He grins and narrows his blue eyes, thinking.

Last night was amazing and now I have the Presidential nomination. I know that I'm going to run this country and the world. Humanity has no clue that their days of freedom are numbered. I'm going to own every single soul and that damn-well includes hell. I'm the Dark Prince and I'll be damned if I don't take my place in this world. I will make this world my domain and every single human my servant. Nobody can stop me.

Lyon shudders and a hot heat spreads through his body. His skin reacts to Sorath's evil energy.

What the fuck. I can hear him, that bastard. He's been born. And, fuck! He's grown. Nobody stopped this from happening. I don't have my powers. I'm the only one that knows this? I need to get to my Citadel and hell. I need to get help.

Sorath looks around the gas station, squinting his eyes. He turns to the right and left, scowling. He narrows his eyes to focus across the street.

I can't see him but I feel him. What the fuck! Who is it? I know he has some powers if he can mask his presence but I still can feel him. I can feel a demon but I can't see him. That's fucking odd!

He turns to look at Lyon. *Hell, it can't be that guy, he doesn't have the aura. I can't see his eyes because of the shades. Fuck!* He shrugs and turns away.

Lyon looks at him, not reacting to his stare.

This is fucked up! He's looking at me and that means that he feels me. He looks confused. Yeah, he can't recognize me, my aura. That's why I've been able to survive out in the world these thousands of years.

Hell, he can't see who I am. My powers are low but the orb protects me from being detected. I can't fucking believe this. I need to do something. I can't even reach out to the Archangels. Fuck!

Sorath takes the nozzle from the car and returns it to its slot. He closes the gas tank with the cap. He then opens the car door and slides into the black leather seat.

Fuck, where is that damn demon? He looks at the time and shrugs.

I need to get going, I have the meeting with the FBI Director Ice.

He pulls out of the gas station and onto the street. The BMW speeds away down the street.

Lyon narrows his eyes to read the license plate. He turns to grab the gas nozzle from his truck and places it in its slot. He replaces the gas cap and slams the door shut.

He turns around to open the truck's door. He places his hand on the door handle ready to pull it open. He's feels a strong pull to look at the mural across the parking lot.

He stares at the painting and the rows of glyphs. The painting has different generations of Mexicans, depicting different eras of their history. The mural has a tall muscular Aztec with long black hair, holding a stone tablet with his two hands. The stone tablet has rows and rows of glyphs.

Lyon looks at the glyphs and starts to read the tablet frowning.

"What is this? I can read those glyphs? Hell, that's unreal."

He squints his eyes to focus on the glyphs, frowning. He grabs the car door handle with his right hand as he reads the tablet.

"The world has several portals that open into the deep dark Citadel and realms of hell. The portals are accessible twice a day, at the moment of the unique time of twilight. The moment between dawn and sunrise and sunset and dusk.

"Read the galactic signs and follow your heart. Unlock your mind to the old, the now, and the new. The new world's culture will open the doors to your destiny. Follow the direction and the signals.

"The entrance to the cave is the portal to the realms. You have the twilight time to access the portal. The portal nearby is El Matador. This portal will take you to your quest. Heed the signs and listen to your heart."

Lyon continues to read the glyphs and over again. *Can this be true? Are the directives for me? I need to check this out in case they are.*

He pulls out his cell phone from his pants. He quickly enters El Matador in the search bar. The address, map, and images pop up. His fingers slide over the screen to look at the images. He slowly starts to grin.

"I'm going to go there tonight at twilight. I'm going to see if this spot is the portal and I can get into hell. Fucking sweet!"

He slides his cell back into his pants and opens the truck's door.

I need to get something to eat because my energy is low. Yeah, I don't have to eat everyday but I do need to eat or drink some blood. I don't have time to look for blood. It's too dangerous in this time period in the human world.

The diner is crowded with families. The young children are laughing, yelling, or crying. The floor is covered in food or spilled soda.

Crystal walks around the tables towards the bar counter. She looks around the room and shrugs. She slides onto the bar stool and leans both elbows on the counter. She looks at the waitress running around like crazy behind the counter.

Oh dear, she's looks exhausted and ready to explode.

Crystal raises her hands to push back her long black hair behind her ears. She turns to look at the waitress again and starts to tap her fingers on the counter.

I'm getting really nervous because I've been feeling this ominous gut wrenching feeling for no good reason. I don't like it. I didn't have any breakfast or lunch, and I'm forcing myself to have dinner. Hell, I should just walk out and grab a hamburger.

She turns around and slides off the stool and walks around the tables and small children. She smiles weakly at them and walks out of the diner's glass door.

She stops a few steps away from the door and inhales deeply, closing her eyes. Her hands shake and she looks around her.

Oh hell, I don't see anything or anyone scary. What's up?

She shakes her head and turns to walk down the street towards the Hamburger R Us at the corner.

She walks inside and orders her hamburger, fries, and soda. She takes the order number and walks towards a table on the side of the room.

She slides onto the chair and waits for her order to be delivered. She turns to look out into the ocean.

Yes, this is a beautiful time in the early evening. I might stay to see the sunset. I love to see it every chance I get and that's not often because of my work schedule. I love the short drive from the city. I'm happy that I have three days off.

She raises one hand and rests her chin in her open palm. She sighs deeply, smiles, and starts to relax.

Her cell flashes an image of the sender. She looks at it with her finger hovering over the screen.

Should I respond or not? I'm trying to relax and hell, my twin always gets me uptight. She's the reason that I moved to the west coast to get away from her constant drama. We're so different yet we look identical. Hell, she's high maintenance and I'm much more casual.

I want a family and she wants money and fun. Oh yeah, and lots of hunks.

I wonder what she wants now, yes, her name is Crystal Ivonne and I'm Crystal Ivette. It's great that she likes to be called Cryssi because having the same first name sucks. I'm going to ignore her for now because I want to eat in peace. I'll talk to her later.

She smiles and looks out into the ocean. She taps the phone to shut it down.

A few moments later, she taps on the phone again to read her favorite book. She sides her finger over the screen and reads about myths, gods, fallen angels, and demons.

"Oh gosh, those names are different and some are fascinating. I wonder if I could learn more about them."

The black limestone is saturated with the fresh red blood. The only sound in the room is the hiss from the flogging whip moving through the air and landing on the Samyaza's smooth healed back.

Samyaza's body is full of energy and is regenerating quickly, keeping up with the constant damage from the flogging.

He opens his violet eyes and they glow with the strong energy aura. He closes his eyes to focus.

I need to try to connect with Apollyon because I know that he could release me. I know that he has the power to do so. I'm a little concerned that he hasn't responded to my calls. It's been a long time and it's very odd.

I know that he's alive because I can feel his aura but not strong. Lucifer also feels him the same as I do. That's why I asked him. I thought it was me but now I know for sure it's Apollyon.

Apollyon! Hear me and help me out! Come and release me from this punishment!

Apollyon! Answer me! Don't ignore my pleas!

Samyaza opens his brilliant violet eyes, searching the room for him.

Fuck! He's not responding. I'll try again later and I'll keep on trying as long as I have energy.

The evil demons flash into the corner of the room to watch him suffer. They take pleasure in his suffering.

"Rasp, go faster!"

The big, wide black demon lisps. His rotten teeth are missing in the front. His black eyes excitedly move right and left.

Samyaza glares at them. "You rotten feces! Fuck off! I'm not your entertainment."

The demons chuckle and clasp their claws together. They huddle in the corner, nodding.

"We have every right to be here because this is our realm. We pay to see you and you're our favorite fallen angel. We love your violet eyes when they glow."

The tall demon yells at Samyaza, smiling wide and flashing the double row of pointed teeth. The shorter demon nods and takes a couple steps forward.

"I love watching you, my love. I love every single detail about you. I especially love watching your cock because it looks so mouthwateringly delicious. Can I have a taste?"

The demon smiles and bats her eyes. She places her right hand on her waist and twirls around.

Samyaza shudders, not from the pain but from intense revulsion.

"I can't fucking believe it! You're a female demon! What the fuck!!"

She nods and smiles at him, placing both hands on her waist and nodding. She winks, tilting her head from right to left, and smiles at him.

Four

The tide is low and slow clashing over the rocks at the entrance of the unique cave, El Matador. This cave is located in Southern California, a few miles down the coast, in the Los Angeles area.

The sun is slowly setting, casting a beautiful dazzling red orange display of color over the sea.

Crystal walks inside the cave and wades through the water to the back of the cave. She climbs to sit up high, on a huge rock, waiting for the sunset. She leans against the rock and the waves smash against the rocks, rushing inside the cave.

Crystal pulls her legs up against her chest and smiles. Her beautiful face is relaxed and flushed a soft rosy shade, and her eyes sparkle.

I can't wait to see the sunset and then I'm going to go home and relax. Maybe I'll drink some wine and listen to music. Tomorrow I'll go watch a movie. Yeah, then I'll read after I finish my errands.

A soft breeze blows inside the cave, wrapping her hair around her. She moves her right hand up and pushes a strand out of her eyes.

Her eyes open wide when she sees Apollyon walk towards the cave. She bites her lower lip and doesn't move.

She watches him closely. She scoots back further behind the rocks. She's curious to see what's he's doing with a Glock.

Lyon walks over the rocks, fully dressed for action. He has his modern weapon, his Glock, tucked inside his waist band.

He ties the black leather cord tight and walks towards the cave's entrance.

He twists his head to each side, scrutinizing the cave.

"Hell, this place is amazing. I should return and enjoy the beach."

He stands in the entrance and turns to look at the sunset, waiting for the special moment in time, the twilight.

He squints his eyes to focus out into the horizon, clenching his hands into fists.

"Fuck, this is it. I really want this to work because I don't know any other way to get in."

The sky turns a faint color of gray and the cave entrance appears to flicker and appears like a mirror. The mirror appears to be liquefied.

"Yes, fuck yes!"

Lyon pushes his fist through the mirror and sees it disappear.

"I'm going in because I don't have a clue how long this portal is open. I need to start the alarm because inside Hell I won't know what the time it is in the world."

He clicks the alarm and takes a step inside the mirror. He takes a step into hell.

Crystal eyes open wider and she moves down the rocks. *What happened to him? Where did he go? I need to pull him back. This is crazy, unreal. Did I really see him disappear? Did he fall and the waves are pulling into the ocean?*

"God, It's get darker and I missed the sunset!"

She stops at the spot where Lyon was standing. She moves her hand as she turns to look around.

Her hand enters the portal and then the portal disappears.

"Gawd, what was that?" She moves her hand in the area that it happened.

"I must be crazy." She frowns and looks around her and out into rocks.

"I can't see him and I didn't bring my flashlight. Did I really see him disappear into… what? Geeze, this is so crazy but I know that my hand went inside and disappeared for a moment. I felt the heat. This is crazy!"

He stands at the portal and slowly turns around. The cave is chilling, pitch black and fine mist envelops him. His eyelashes are instantly wet and clump together. His long, black hair is soaked and his leather pants and jacket are wet. He squints his beautiful, swirling gray-blue eyes to look through the mist.

I'm in, but where? I can't believe it but I don't remember or know my way to my domain, the Citadel. I'm going to search for the entrance of my domain in this hell-hole. I know it's in a different dimension but how do I access my portal? I don't know if I have the power to get in! Fuck! This is insane. What the fuck is my mission? Why now? The scripture on the mural said that I have a quest.

Fuck, why not be up front and direct? I have to unscramble this puzzle.

He places his hands on his hips turning around. "Fuck! It's so damn dark that I can't see where the opening to the tunnel is."

He takes a step forward to search for the entrance to the tunnel. He continues walking on wet black limestone. He enters the first station of hell. He stops and looks at several piles of skeletons on the floor.

"Fuck, I don't remember this station because I only visited the ninth station of hell, near my abyss, where the Watchers are imprisoned in their special station. I know that Sam is in another station being punished because he was the leader of the fallen."

He walks forward and stumbles as he trips over a rock. He reaches out to break his fall. He lands on his back next to the pile of skeletons and stares up. He blinks several times as he looks at the red demons staring at him.

Their black eyes shimmer and their dark red wrinkled skin flickers fire. They look like red round jelly balls. The demons are the Furies' demons that guard the first station of hell. They hold onto the black limestone with their claws.

Their rotten, pointed, double-row teeth are sharp. Their round jaws start to move in a fast, croaky chatter. The demons watch Lyon closely, their huge eyes spin in their sockets.

The Furies demons don't recognize him since his powers are bound. They feel a slight energy aura.

What the fuck! They don't recognize me and I sure as hell don't recognize them. I know that they're demons.

He moves slowly to sitting position and swiftly jumps up. He glares at them.

"Fuck off!"

The heavy Furies demon screeches and jumps on Apollyon. He wraps his round arms around Apollyon's neck, to pull him down with him.

"You're in our station!"

"Fuck you!"

Apollyon moves fast and bends over, throwing the demon over his shoulders and onto the wet ground.

He takes long several steps, walking around from the Furies demon on the ground.

"We're not going to allow you to enter the first station of hell. We won't allow you to disturb the souls in limbo."

The thinner Furies demon falls down from the wall, onto the ground next to Apollyon. He attacks Lyon with his hands and teeth. The other demons follow him.

One demon bites into his shoulder, tearing the leather jacket with his sharp, pointed teeth.

"What the fuck!"

Apollyon raises his arms up over his head and quickly turns around in a circle to dislodge the foul-smelling Furies demon.

"Get the fuck away from me! I'm your master!"

The Furies demons chuckle and rant around him in croaky voices.

"Master, you're not. Food you are. We're hungry. Sweet meat, sweet meat! You're ours."

They flash at once to land on him and he falls onto the ground and rolls over, shoving some off him.

"Get the fuck back!"

Lyon yells and pulls out his Glock. He fires one bullet into the demon near him.

The fat Furies demon falls backward and rolls on the ground. A stream of florescent green blood flows out of his stomach.

"Ahhhhhhhh…….ohhhhhh…..Sizzzzzzaaaazzz…."

Lyon looks around the cave, taking advantage of the faint illumination that the blood provides. *Fuck I see the tunnel.*

The Furies demons turn to look at the green blood running down the demon's huge stomach. They hiss and flash over to Lyon to attack.

They latch on to his body with their sharp teeth to bring Lyon down.

Lyon inhales deeply and uses his limited power to turn around in a circle like a whirlwind. The force of the spin forces them to lose their grip on his limps.

"Fuck off!!"

The Furies demons fly through the air and crash into the side limestone walls and onto the ground. They explode like water balloons. The Furies demons molecules rush to bond into their shape. Then they lie on the ground, dazed from the impact.

Apollyon starts to run towards what appears to be the entrance to the tunnel. His neck and hands are bleeding dark, florescent-red blood.

Damn it, I don't heal as quickly as I used to. It's going to take a little longer to heal these damn wounds. Damn them! Hell, I hope this is the route inside. I have to look out for more demons since they don't recognize me. Damn it!

He runs down the tunnel, suddenly losing his balance, and rolling down the steps. He bangs his head into the limestone wall.

"Damn!"

He yells, closing his eyes as he rolls into a fetal position. He bounces down the steep staircase for what feels like an eternity. He lands at the bottom in a pool of cold water.

"Fuck! This is not my day. Damn it! I still don't know where I'm going or what my quest is."

He jumps back when the side of the walls flare up into flames, scorching the walls. The flames die out after a minute. He frowns and looks around the long tunnel.

Damn, at least it's not pitch black and I can see something.

He walks down the tunnel, looking for more Furies demons. He holds his Glock in his hand ready to shoot. He walks a few feet and the walls erupt into flames again. He jumps away from the fire, frowning.

"Damn it! They must erupt every couple of minutes. Hell!"

He looks down the tunnel as far as he can see. Then the fire dies out. He shrugs and walks forward and he trips on the step down. He rolls down the tunnel in a ball.

He reaches the bottom of the rocky tunnel, face-down. He lies on his stomach for a few seconds. *Hell, that was something else.*

"Having limited powers sucks! What the fuck do I need to do to get my powers back?"

He moves his arms and places his hands on the ground. He pushes up, looking around the huge cavity. Then the side of the walls flare up with flames, the flames raging up from the bottom of the pit. The fiery light envelops the walls and the rock pillars.

"That's incredible. It looks like a fire pit. Fuck! I don't remember this place."

He stares at the bridge that crosses the vast expanse to the other side. His eyes roam, taking in the sharp odd-shaped rock pillar formations that originate from the bottom of the pit. The rock pillars are formed in such a way that they creates a bridge. Some of the rocks are spaced out wider than others.

"I can make it. I'm not completely without my powers. I only have very little use of them. Fuck! I wish I could flash over to the other side."

He takes the jump onto the first rock pillar, trying to balance as he lands on the uneven surface and he squats. The flames erupt again. He looks up to see how high the flames reach.

"Damn, it's fucking amazing. Look at all those souls floating up above. Yeah, they do look like they're in limbo. I think that this is the first station of hell. I never bothered to check out the different stations of hell."

He looks at the souls swirling around up in the vast expanse.

Samyaza grinds his teeth, closing his beautiful violet eyes when the flogger lands on his back once again.

"Fuck!"

He yells out in pain. He lays his head back, every muscle flexing as his body tenses from the flogging. His back instantly heals.

"Damn, I have to reach Apollyon! I'm going to call him before my energy gets depleted from this flogging."

Apollyon! Please answer me. I implore you to release me. You were going to the last time that you were here. I know that you were. Where are you? Release me!

"Hell!"

Samyaza yells out and glares at the Demons in the corner, laughing.

"Fuck you!"

The demons' bodies jiggle like jelly as they chuckle. Their black eyes shine and frothy green saliva runs down their chins.

Lyon takes a leap and lands on the next rock pillar formation. He lands on his two feet, bending his knees to cushion the jump. His huge body tenses as the fire erupts around him.

"Fuck! I'm going to get cooked in here. That means that I only have a couple of minutes between the fire eruptions to jump."

He looks at the souls floating up high and then he looks down at the infinite fire pit. Lyon moves his arms and places his hands on his waist as he looks across the fire at the limestone wall. His eyes widen when he sees some glyphs.

"The virtues are your ally. Courage is a virtue that will be rewarded. Listen to you heart, open your mind, and trust your instinct. Thy journey has been written, thy quest is near, and thou shalt succeed over the Dark Prince."

What the hell does this mean? I hate these riddles that I have to decipher them.

"Could this be about that evil bastard that I met this morning at the station? He did refer to himself as the Dark Prince. Fucking crazy!"

Lyon scowls and squints his beautiful, swirling gray-blue eyes. *What the hell does this mean?* He opens his eyes and he looks over to the wall again.

"Fuck, it's gone! Did I imagine it?"

He turns to look at the next rocky pillar. He clenches his hands into fists and sighs.

"Damn! That pillar looks small."

He grinds his molars, squinting his eyes. Lyon inhales deeply and takes the leap. He lands on the rock pillar with one foot on the pillar and the other foot half way on the rock. He tips back and he quickly tips forward, balancing his weight. Instantly, he falls onto his knees and his Glock slides out of his waistband, bounces across the rock and stops at the edge. He leans forward and grabs the Glock. He looks down into the deep fire pit, shaking his head.

"Damn! That was close. How in the world do the humans take such risks hiking? I'm immortal but I don't know if I would survive that scorching fire pit."

His hair comes loose from the black leather cord, flowing down around his shoulders.

The fire pit erupts and flames dance around him.

"Apollyon!"

Lyon startles, looks around and gets up from his knees. He turns to look across to the other side.

"I know I heard someone calling me."

He jumps to the next two rocky pillars. He stops and waits for the fire to die down.

"Apollyon! Don't ignore my pleas."

Lyon frowns and looks around the fire pit. He shrugs his big shoulders, shakes his head.

I know that's Samyaza but I can't communicate. I have to hurry and release him. I need his help. I know that I need to release him and the others. We need to take down the Dark Prince. I felt his powers and they're growing.

"Samyaza, where are you?"

Lyon turns around, searching for him. He jumps at the next rocky pillar and waits for the fire to stop.

"Fuck, that's another pillar that has a wider space."

He waits for the fire to die down and he grinds his molars and takes the leap. He lands on the pillar, right in the center, swaying to balance his weight.

"I'm almost halfway across and I need to hurry."

Lyon leaps across the rocks, waiting out the fire eruptions. He reaches the other side, grinning.

"Yeah, made it."

Lyon turns around and walks to the entrance of the tunnel. He walks down the incline in the tunnel which makes a sharp turn down a rocky stairway. He reaches the end of the stairway and looks at the bridge.

This is a real bridge, cut from the black limestone. The bridge has an intricate pattern on the rails. The pattern looks like skulls, roses, and crosses intertwined with vines. The crosses have deep red rubies incrusted in the center of the cross.

He stops at the entrance of the bridge to touch the beautiful intricate pattern of the rail.

"Damn, this is beautiful work."

He nods, then he takes a step onto the bridge. Instantly he feels the strong vortex, circling through the station. His hair wraps around his neck and he holds on tight to the rail. He squints to watch the souls punished as they are being blown around in the vortex.

"Fuck! Will I make it across the bridge?"

He squats to gain some small amount of protection from the rails, and moves slowly toward the other side.

"I have to find a faster means to Samyaza. I know that he's near my domain. Yeah, in a different dimension. That's not going to help me. Damn it!"

"Apollyon!"

"Fuck, where are you, Sam?"

Apollyon stops in the middle of the bridge to listen. He leans on the rail to look down.

"Fuck! That's a deep black chasm."

He shakes his head and continues across the bridge. He enters another station.

"I can't believe that I can't locate my Master! It's been thousands of years since I've seen him. He left without a word."

Rakshasi is Apollyon's personal female demon, who shapeshifts. He calls her Shasi and he doesn't remember her.

Shasi wanders in the Citadel searching for Apollyon. She walks along the black marble hallway towards the throne room.

She's wearing a deep red gown which ties on one shoulder, exposing the other shoulder. The edge of the material is embroidered with a half inch of silver thread. A wide silver ribbon is wrapped below her breasts. The material flows loosely down to her thighs.

She walks down the marble floor. Her long legs extend and she places her feet onto the marble floor, creating a soft tapping sound. Her silver sandals straps wrap up her leg. .

Her long shiny black hair is braided with silver ribbon, woven into the single ponytail. The wide three inch silver band holds her hair up high on the crown of her head. Her fangs shine brightly as they extend from her gums and rest on her full red lips.

"I'm hungry, but I have to search for my Master."

She walks towards Apollyon's crystal sphere to look for him. Her ponytail swings across her bottom. She stops in front of the round pedestal, which is located next to the altar. She places her hands on the edge of the marble table and looks into the sphere.

The sphere swirls with a silver and red color until someone looks into it.

Her huge red-specked topaz eyes gaze into the sphere, searching for him.

"Every day I search for my Master, but he's not here. I need to go into the hell realm to search for him there. I want to help him because I know that he needs me. I'm so worried. I love attending my Master."

Shasi is dejected. She sighs and leans forward to stare into the crystal sphere. Her long lashes touch her delicately arched eyebrows as her eyes widen with surprise.

"Is that my Master? He looks so different with those clothes on. He looks confused. He's in one of the Hell stations. I'm going to help him!"

Shasi runs out of the throne room, down the hallway. She turns to the right down the long corridor. She enters her room and walks out onto the balcony. She snaps her fingers and the gown falls to her feet in a red pool of silk. She instantly shifts into a huge red dragon with black-silver wings. She exhales black and red fire and emits her silver iridescent smoke.

I have to go into hell, to the third station.

Shasi magically flashes into the other parallel dimension, Hell. She flies up through the stations through the access holes.

Lyon walks into the next station and stops to look at the beautiful clear water fall. The water falls into the pool in the center of the vast station.

The souls desperately attempt to climb onto the rocks. The icy storm and wind knocks them over into the icy cold pool.

"What the fuck!"

He crosses his arms and grinds his molars. *I'm supposed to swim across? Fuck!*

"Lyon! What's taking you so long? I'm done here! I heard you!"

Samyaza yells out before the flogger lands on his back again. His body tenses as the flogger cuts deep into his flesh.

"Damn, Sam! I'm trying to get to you!"

Shasi flies into the strong rain and wind. She squints her clear topaz eyes, the red specks flash. She's trying to keep the water from pounding into her eyes. She angrily shrieks, exhales her red and black fire, and flies over to Apollyon, emitting her silver iridescent smoke.

Lyon raises his eyes amazed and slowly smiles. *Damn, that's a dragon! I don't remember dragons.*

Hell, I don't remember a lot and yet I remember some stuff, like I'm an angel and I have brothers that are imprisoned in hell. I know why but I don't know why my powers are bound.

Shasi lands next to Lyon and instantly shifts and snaps her fingers to don her dress. She raises her arms, outstretched straight, and she places her right hand on top of her left hand and she bows her head.

"Master Apollyon, I'm here to aid you."

Lyon frowns, perplexed and he raises his right eyebrow.

"Yah? Who are you?"

Shasi raises her head and lowers her arms. She stands straight and tall.

"Master Apollyon, I'm your Rakshasi. I'm your faithful warrior, and I attend to your needs."

Lyon narrows his eyes. His eyes roam her perfect body, and he frowns.

"You're my faithful warrior? That's ridiculous. Why would I need you when I have powers?"

Well, hmm……I do have powers. Damn it. She looks beautiful and fragile. She attends to my needs?

She stands tall and motionless, waiting for him to speak. Only the red specks in her topaz eyes sparkle.

"Master, I've been your Rakshasi since I was a tot. You rescued me from the other Rakshasi attack when I became an orphan."

Lyon eyebrows rise up as he frowns, his lips compressed tightly. He shakes his head.

Damn it! I have her in my domain and she's my warrior. Damn!

"Do you have a name?"

Shasi smiles and nods, flashing her fangs.

"Master, you call me Shasi."

"Oh………that sounds good. So, you're a dragon?"

Shasi shakes her head and shrugs. "I'm a shifter. I can shift into anything I want but I love the dragon the best. I also have powers."

"Oh, so your true form is female?"

Shasi grins. She nods vigorously, shaking her long ponytail around her head.

"Yes Master. I came to aid you. Would you care for me to take you to the Citadel?"

"Lyon!"

Apollyon nods and moves his head up. He yells out.

"I'm coming, Sam! Give me a few. It's not easy!"

"What the fuck! What's so damn difficult?"

"I have to get to your cell. I don't know how!" Lyon glances over at Shasi. He raises his right eyebrow.

"What?"

Lyon ignores Sam and crosses his arms. He grinds his jaw to control his frustration and pride.

"Shasi, could you help me get to Samyaza?"

Shasi smiles and nods her head. "Yes, Master. I'll be happy to take you to him."

"Right."

He waits for her to tell him how.

Shasi snaps her fingers and her clothes disappear and she instantly shifts into the dragon.

Her dragon wings spread out wide, fifty feet on each side. She looks at him, and exhales some black and red fire.

"Master, jump on my back.

Lyon looks at her back and the sharp scales that run down her back.

"Right."

She moves her head like she did in her human form. She blinks several times and shrieks.

"Ok! I'm getting on!"

Lyon jumps up and grabs onto a scale and pulls himself up onto her back. He holds onto a scale and looks around the station.

"I'm ready."

Shasi exhales her black and red fire and flies away from the station. She flies through tunnels, around mountains, and the stations of Hell.

Lyon holds onto the scale. He looks around, trying to recognize a station… or anything. *Damn, I can't remember a thing but I know that I've been here before.*

She finally reaches the fallen angels' punishment station.

Lyon looks at the fallen angel station, which looks different from the other Hell stations. He frowns and looks around. *This station only has a titanium door, but I bet it's locked.*

She stops next to the ledge of the station entrance. Her wings flap and she emits her silver iridescent smoke.

Lyon moves his right leg over the scale and jumps onto the ledge. He balances and turns to look at her.

"Wait here, because I want you to take me to the portal."

Shasi shrieks and nods her head. She turns into her human form and snaps her fingers to dress. She waves her hand and the door opens.

Lyon blinks and nods. "Wait here."

"Yes, Master." She stands tall and straight next to the door in her deep red dress and sandals.

Five

The entrance to the fallen angel's imprisonment station is dark and cold. Apollyon walks down the tunnel with his hands out to avoid running into the wall. He stumbles, spreads his arms out to the sides to gain his balance.

"This is fucking unreal! It's fucking dark in here. I can't see anything!"

He walks slowly and he walks into the wall. He turns to the right with his arms extended.

"Lyon!! Where are you?"

Samyaza yells before the flogging. He grinds his molars and his body tenses. The deep gouges on his back bleed. The blood runs down his back, down his ass, and down his legs.

"Hell Sam, I'm here in this fucking dark station. I'm almost there!"

Sam's energy is depleted and he faints before he hears Apollyon. The flogger keeps on with the steady flogging. Sam's back is raw, totally shredded.

Lyon turns the corner and the tunnel's firelights, hanging from the high ceiling, light up.

Lyon blinks rapidly to adjust to the light. He takes long strides down the long hall and reaches a spiral stairway down.

"Hell, this is crazy! I don't remember this stairway."

He takes careful steps onto the next narrow step. He scowls when the stone step edge crumbles. He leans back into the wall and slowly looks over the edge of the stairway. He looks down to see how long it is.

"Fuck! I can break my neck going down this stairway."

He takes the next steps and nods. The steps are solid. He moves a little faster down the steps, hugging the wall. A couple of steps crumble and the rocks fall down the side.

"Damn it!"

He takes a few minutes to reach the dungeon, the fallen angels' captivity cells.

He looks into the small opening in each titanium door. Most of the cells are empty but some have fallen angels.

"Sam!"

I can't hear him and his energy aura is low. He's nearly spent.

Apollyon looks at the last cell and sees Samyaza, bleeding profusely now.

"Stop that flogging!"

He yells at the station guard. He pushes on the door to open it. It won't open. He looks through the small opening.

The station guard demon stops. He turns his head, and looks at him. He growls at Lyon and walks to the door. He opens the door.

"Fuck off!"

"What the hell! I'm your Master!"

The station guard looks startled and gazes at him. He narrows his eyes and shakes his head.

"You're not!"

The station guard demon, Rasp swings the flogger, and it wraps around Apollyon's left forearm. He pulls the flogger and Lyon falls onto the cold black limestone.

"Damn! I need my powers!"

Lyon yells out. He takes advantage of the flogger wrapped around his arm. He pulls his huge arm back, and tugs the flogger. He pulls down the huge station demon guard.

The guard falls down next to Lyon, surprised. He turns, fisting his huge hand. He swings back his arm, and hits Lyon on the jaw.

Lyon's head rolls back against the stone floor and the guard falls onto Apollyon's chest, ready to continue the attack.

Lyon pushes his pelvis up and throws the guard off him. He rolls and jumps up. He stands with his legs spread apart, glaring at the guard.

"Stop, you dumbs shit!"

The guard smiles. His sharp teeth flash, and he laughs.

"Come to daddy."

"Fuck you, dumb shit!"

Lyon glares at him and jumps up to knock him down. The demon falls back onto his back and rams his head on the black limestone floor.

The demon guard yells a long load throaty sound. He lifts his legs up to wrap around Lyons legs and knocks him of his feet. Lyon falls onto the floor, face down.

The demon jumps on Lyon's back and wraps his huge arm around Apollyon's neck.

Lyon shifts his legs in an attempt to push up and dislodge the demon's arm.

The demon holds Lyon tight and bounces with the shoves.

"Fuck!"

Lyon finally manages to get on his back. He reaches inside his leather jacket to pull out his Glock. He shoves the Glock next to the Demon's heart. He pulls the trigger and the bullet penetrates the Demon's heart.

The Demon's eyes widen, he looks surprised. He relaxes his hold on Apollyon. He then falls onto the ground with green florescent blood gushing out of hole in his chest.

Lyon looks at him and shakes his head.

"You stupid fiend! I'm your Master!"

Lyon turns to look at Samyaza. He runs over to him and touches his neck with his fingers to check his pulse.

"Oh fuck! He's almost gone! That means that he didn't get enough nourishment to keep him charged. Damn it! He's bleeding and not regenerating!"

Lyon moves his hands along his back to heal him. The shredded flesh starts to heal slowly. Lyon shakes his head.

I have to hurry and get him down and out of this cell. I need to feed him.

Lyon looks at the wall and frowns. His eyes read the inscription on the wall.

"Courage is a virtue that will be rewarded."

Lyon's body glows a bright red as a segment of restrained energy aura is released. He looks at his aura. He deeply inhales then exhales, closing his eyes.

Yes, I can feel my power ramp up, I feel stronger. Is that what that scripture means? Could it be authentic and the only means to regain my powers?

He opens his eyes and closes his hands, flexing the muscles on his arms. He moves his hands over the silver cuffs and the cuffs open.

Sam falls into Lyon's huge strong arms. Lyon catches him and swings him over his shoulder. He moves his hands over the cuffs on his ankles. The cuffs releases Sam's ankles.

"Yes!"

Lyon turns around and walks out of the door. He starts to run down the hall with Sam on his right shoulder, holding him tight with his right arm.

Sam back has stopped bleeding but he's still drained. I need to get him some blood or food to revitalize him but I need to get him out of Hell.

Lyon turns the corner and retraces his steps back to the entrance. The extra increment of power has increased his strength and abilities.

He reaches the door and stops. He looks over at Shasi and leans down. He slides Sam off his shoulder and onto the ground.

He opens his teeth and extends his fangs, seeing Sam's color turn grey.

"Fuck!"

"Master, I could help."

Shasi walks over to them and waits for his direction.

"Shasi, get ready to take us out of Hell!"

"Yes, Master."

Shasi snaps her fingers and her clothes disappear and instantly turns into her dragon. She flaps her huge wings and hovers near the ledge, waiting for Lyon. She watches his every move.

Lyon falls down onto his knees. He bites into the vein on his right wrist, and his dark rich blood spurts out. He places his wrist over Sam's mouth and slides his left hand under Sam's neck.

The blood squirts into his mouth, and slides down his throat.

"Samyaza! Wake up, brother! Drink some of my blood."

Samyaza remains motionless and unresponsive. Lyon anxiously moves his wrist over Sam's lips.

"Sam! I need your help! Come on and drink up!"

Apollyon moves his head with his fingers to wake him.

Sam's color slowly turns white with a faint hint of pink.

"Yes! Drink up, brother."

Sam opens his mouth and he extracts more of Lyon's blood. A couple of minutes later, he opens his beautiful violet eyes. His eyes are dull and bloodshot. He stops drinking and closes his eyes, exhausted. Lyon pulls his wrist away and licks up his wounds.

"Hey, are you ready to leave?"

Samyaza's color is slowly returning but he still looks pale. He nods, opening his eyes and his lips turn up at the corners. He's too weak to speak.

Lyon stands, taking Sam in his arms and turns to Shasi as he slides him over his right shoulder.

"Shasi, get us out of Hell!"

Shasi squeaks. She exhales her red and black fire. She flaps her wings, emitting her silver iridescent smoke. Her huge topaz eyes blink rapidly, eager to aid Lyon.

Lyon slides his left leg onto her back and holds on to her scale with his left hand to pull himself onto her back. He holds on tight to Samyaza.

Shasi flies through the stations of Hell. She swoops into the tunnels and out into the thunder, soaking Lyon and Sam. Her skin sparkles and she blinks to clear the huge raindrops. The fire pits dries them up and sears Lyon and Sam. She then flies over the fiery boiling water. She dives, twirls, and soars through stations to get to the portal.

The demons in each station fly after them. Some continue their pursuit and the others stay in their station to guard.

"The Bolgle demon is close, Shasi! We need to lose him and the Furies."

Shasi dips her head down and flies down like a torpedo through the air to reach the abyss. She swoops to the right and flies up, making them crash into each other. She squeaks and flies to the station above to the portal.

She flies over the rocky pillars and stops next to the ledge. She flaps her wings and hovers to allow Lyon to slide off. She exhales her red and black fire burning the Furies that are clutching the wall near the portal.

"Hell, yes! Shasi, your fire is stronger than theirs! That was a fucking cool move!"

Shasi squeaks and blinks her huge topaz eyes. The red sparks flicker. She hovers near the ledge to protect Lyon and to keep the other Furies away.

The Furies hiss and they talk in unison in their croaky voices.

"Damn, their constant chatter can drive you insane!"

Lyon turns to glare at the thousands of Furies flying over the fire pit.

He walks to the portal. He places Sam on the ground and pulls out his cell. He looks at the time.

"Damn it, we have some time to kill! I wanted to get him out of Hell and home. I want to attend to his injuries because they're taking a long time to regenerate."

He looks at the portal and clenches his jaw. He turns to gaze at Shasi, exhaling fire at the Furies to keep them away.

"Shasi, we have some time to wait. How long can you keep this up?"

Shasi squeaks and flaps her wings. She blinks rapidly and nods her head.

"Yeah, right. I totally understand! Hell, was that a little?"

Shasi squeaks and shakes her head again. She exhales more fire.

"Yeah, got it! Not!"

Lyon turns around and runs his fingers through his long hair. He looks at Samyaza's naked body and shrugs off his leather jacket.

He slides his jacket onto Sam's left arm, pulling the jacket gently across the wounds on his back, and slides his right arm into the sleeve.

"Fuck, his color looks a lot better but he's not restored. Sam only has enough potency to keep him alive but he's still hurt. I wished that I had my powers back. I only gained some of my strength. Damn it!"

Moments later, Lyon pulls out his cell phone and looks at the time.

"Yeah, it's almost time, only a couple minutes more."

Apollyon gathers Samyaza in his arms to be ready to step into the portal the moment that twilight starts.

He looks at the entrance, waiting for the portal to open up.

"Apollyon! What the fuck are you doing?"

Lucifer yells from across the tunnel. He's standing on the ledge with his hands clinched at this sides. His beautiful blue eyes shine brightly and he moves back his arm to discharge a fire bolt at Lyon.

"Samyaza is not allowed to leave my realm! Don't force me to stop you!"

Apollyon growls. He looks down at Samyaza, and he clenches his jaw, flexing his jaw muscle. His amazing swirling gray-blue eyes flash brightly.

"Not happening Luc! I have to release him. It has been written, and it shall be done!"

Lucifer narrows his eyes to focus on Apollyon's aura.

Damn, he's not charged to his full capacity. That's so odd. That's why I couldn't track him. That means that I'm stronger and can overpower him.

Lucifer snarls at him and throws a fire bolt at his feet to force him to cede to his command.

"Don't force me to fight you, Apollyon! I know that you don't have your full strength!"

Lyon growls, he emits his red and black florescent smoke. His fangs extend and his horns start to merge from his temple.

"Arggg…….errrr!"

Lyon growls, his face turning red and his eyes glow.

Sam opens his beautiful violet eyes. He weakly looks up at Lyon. He whispers in a hoarse voice.

"Do….n't leave meee ….here."

The portal flickers, liquefies, and opens up. Lyon nods, and takes a step forward into the door. He leans out into the world and he places Sam outside the portal onto the flat rock, sand, and waves.

"Samyaza, I'm going to talk to Lucifer. Wait right here. I'll return. I know that the portal will remain open for a few minutes."

Lyon looks down at him, nods, and turns around. He and walks down the tunnel. The portal door stays open.

🙢

"Yes Sis, I'll pick you up at the airport next month. I told you that I'll ask for the day off to make sure to be available. Give Mom and Dad a huge hug and kiss."

Crystal grins and her beautiful eyes sparkle happily. Her cute dimples flash enticingly. She laughs and ends the call. She places her cell on the nightstand in her room.

"I'm going to change into shorts because I'm going to go to the Matador cave. I spent all morning doing research about that cave. I wanted to see if anyone has ever seen what I did. I must be crazy because I didn't find a thing!"

She opens her drawer and pulls out a black tank top and black shorts. She grabs her silk shirt and pulls it up over her head. She then unsnaps her bra and frees her huge firm breasts.

She looks in the mirror and smiles. "Yes, I know that I shouldn't do this but I want to feel free and relaxed. Nobody will be there."

She pulls on her tank top and she looks in the mirror. She smiles as she adjusts the tank top over her breasts.

She then pulls up her short black shorts over her small black thong.

"Oh wow, I feel so sexy and hot. I never do this but maybe I should. I never have time to dress sexy or pretty since I'm always working. I don't need to go out on a date to dress sexy."

She reaches for her small silver hoops on her dresser and slides the hoops into her earlobes.

She turns around and walks out of her bedroom into the small living room.

Crystal slides on her sandals, reaches for her small wallet and grabs her keys.

In no time, she's driving down the beautiful California coast. She turns up the radio and sings along to the songs bopping her head and flashing her cute dimples.

Her full red lips turn up at the corners and her eyes sparkle happily as she pulls her car into the parking lot near the stairway.

She gets out of her car and turns to look out into the ocean.

"Hell yes, it's beautiful and nobody is here."

She does her special Crystal booty-bop, raising her hands up in the air. Her huge breasts bounce up and strain against the soft material. The ocean breeze softly caresses her and her nipples harden.

The evening is beautiful. The waves crash onto the beach in a slow dance. Crystal walks down the wooden stairway that leads into the amazing Matador cave.

She smiles, raising her face up to feel the soft breeze blow gently across her skin. She inhales deeply, pushing her huge creamy breasts up, and threatening to spill over the soft black cotton tank top.

"I'm glad that I decided to return to the Matador. I know that I must have imagined that handsome man disappear. That's totally insane. I couldn't resist the pull to return. I feel a powerful need to be here. I was going to go to the other beach that I usually go to, but this time I changed my mind at the last minute."

Crystal walks across the sand and onto the beach, looking out into the ocean.

"Gosh, it's so incredible and I can't wait to see the sunset. I missed it yesterday. I'll sit back in the same spot that I did yesterday. I want to take a photo with my cell."

She splashes through the low tide that's rushing through the cave entrance and crashing against the rocks. She pulls out her hairband from her shorts and gathers her long black shiny hair. She pulls the hairband onto her head.

"Yes, nobody is here! I hope that nobody appears. I still don't believe what I did see yesterday. That's unreal. No, no, I'm crazy. That sort of stuff doesn't happen."

She reaches her favorite spot and drops down onto the flat rock. She pulls her legs up to her chest and wraps her arms around them.

Crystal pulls out her cell phone to take a picture of the sunset. She snaps a few and sits back on the rock, smiling.

"Yes, that sunset is amazing. It's almost over and I have to go before it turns dark."

She slides her cell into her shorts pocket and leans back against the rocky wall. She enjoys the beautiful colors and the ocean soft sounds.

"Ok, it's time to go."

She slides across the rock and swings her legs over. She turns around, stops, and her eyes widen, stunned.

Oh wow, it's the giant dude! He's coming from nowhere but that's impossible.

Crystal blinks rapidly to clear her eyes. She looks at Lyon lean forward with Sam in his arms, and watches him situate Sam onto the rock.

Crystal bites her lower lip to keep from yelling out. She crosses her arms under her breasts to control the shuddering.

I can't believe this. These dudes are huge! They're beautiful but I know or I can feel their strong aura. It's very powerful and they have a huge allure.

Her huge eyes stare at Samyaza's beautiful face. She looks at his full lips and the she looks at his long black eyelashes.

I love his face. He's so gorgeous. Oh hell, I feel strange, something about him calls me.

Samyaza inhales deeply then exhales, releasing his alarm. He rests on the rock, and he slides off into the waves. He sinks into the sand and the waves wash over him. He closes his eyes, and starts to tremble.

"Omg, oh gosh! He's drowning! Where did that other giant dude go? He just left him there to drown?"

Crystal rushes over to him to save him and to administer some first aid.

She slides her arms under his and hooks his huge arms with hers and she pulls him out of the ocean. She drags him into the cave until she reaches the higher level.

She falls onto her ass, grasping for air. She looks down into his gorgeous face, resting on her lap.

Samyaza's breathing is shallow and he's shaking uncontrollably.

Crystal slides from under him and turns onto her knees. Her face is flushed and her eyes roam all over him. She starts to administer first aid, CPR. She compresses his chest and then raises his head to give him mouth to mouth breathing.

"Please respond!"

Crystal continues the cycle of compressions and mouth to mouth breathing. Her training and expertise takes over.

"God, please save him!"

Samyaza starts to cough up sea water as he turns onto his side.

"That's it."

Crystal pats his back and pushes back his long black silky hair out of his face.

The sea water flows out. He coughs, and then turns around to sit up, resting his hand behind his back. He opens his beautiful violet eyes and looks up into Crystal's clear hazel eyes.

He blinks several times to clear the sea water out of his eyes.

"Thank you."

His eyes roam all over her face to drink up her beautiful soul.

"Your soul is pure and innocent."

Crystal frowns and sits back, squatting, and rests her hands on her knees. She blushes deeply and moves a shaky hand to push back a lock of hair behind her ear.

"Is that good?"

She licks her lower lip nervously. Her eyes open wide, dominating her entire face. Her long curly eyelashes sweep up to her finely arched eyebrows. Her little nose twitches slightly.

Samyaza's violet eyes start to glow and his lips turn up in a small smile. He nods. He moves his hand up to cup her soft cheek, rubbing his thumb softly against it.

"Yes."

"Are you feeling better? I can call the paramedics."

Samyaza frowns and shakes his head. He moves his thumb to rub her soft full lips. He looks at them and then he looks up at her.

"No, don't call them. I'm weak but I'll be okay as soon as I eat."

"Oh, ok. Would you like me to take you somewhere to get some food? Where did your friend go? He disappeared into thin air."

Samyaza stops rubbing her lip and lifts her face up to gaze into her beautiful eyes.

"Apollyon will be back. He went back to take care of some issues."

"Huh……ok. Where…hmmmm…did he go?"

She looks into his beautiful eyes, falling in deep into his soul. *I feel his soul and it's amazing. I feel his heart beats slowly but how could this be possible?*

Damn! She's truly connecting and merging with my soul. Who is she? Should I tell her the truth? She might not believe me but I feel her. I feel her, she's mine.

"I'm not sure that you would like to know or believe it. What's your name?"

Crystal unconsciously leans into his hand, gazing deeply into his eyes.

"My name is Crystal Bryant. What's yours?"

Samyaza nods and moves his hand into her long black silky hair. "I'm Samyaza."

"Oh…hmm…that's an unusual name. I think I've only heard it once before. It was the name of a fallen angel."

She leaves his eyes to look at his full soft lips and bites her lower lip. *Oh gosh, he's so hot! I know that he's naked and sinfully yummy.*

Samyaza leans in closer to her lips, and closes his eyes. He whispers before stealing a hungry kiss.

"Sweet Crystal."

Oh my, this sexy hunk is kissing me. Damn!

She opens her mouth and she moves her head to the right to allow him more access. She moves her hand up to rest on his huge shoulder.

Samyaza pulls back. His glowing violet eyes gaze into her beautiful hazel eyes. She smiles at him, her face has a soft flush, and her cute dimples flash.

"Sweet Crystal, did you see where my friend went?"

Crystal nods, she turns slightly, and she looks over to the entrance of the cave.

"He disappeared. I don't know how or where he went. I only know that the entrance is magical."

She blushes a deep red, her eyebrows gather in an embarrassed frown, and her eyes look at Samyaza, feeling unsure and crazy. She pushes up with her legs, and rushes towards the entrance. She stops and raises her arm to move it forward. Her hand up to her wrist disappears, and then she urgently pulls it back.

"Yeah, it feels very hot when it disappears but I'm too scared to enter. I don't know where or what it is but this magical entrance disappears at night."

She walks back to him and sits down next to him. She looks at his beautiful naked body and slowly looks up into his face. She bites her lower lip, blushing, and nervously pushes her hair back behind her ears.

Samyaza grins, reaches over to touch her soft cheek, and rubs his thumb on her soft skin.

"Sweet Crystal, you're so lovely. Did he say anything before he left me here?

Crystal smiles at him and nods. She leans in closer to him move her face into his palm.

"Yes, he said that he'll be right back but it's been a while and it's almost dark. I know that when it's night the magical entrance disappears."

Sam nods and looks out into the ocean, thinking. He looks down at his naked body and shakes his head.

I can't stay here all night waiting for Lyon to return, because what if he doesn't return? I can't be out here naked during the day. I don't know what year it is or how the world is, but I'm sure that this is unacceptable.

He turns to look at Crystal and her clothing. His gaze stops at her huge firm breasts and his mouth waters.

Fuck, her breasts look so enticing and those nipples are begging me to taste them. I'm fucking hungry and she's drugging my senses. Damn, I need to focus on getting out of here, not at how she's connecting with my soul.

He shudders and shifts to cover his engorged cock with the jacket.

"Crystal, I'm going to tell you the truth because you deserve to know. I pray that you believe me, but I need you to promise that you won't tell anyone. I'm also going to need your help."

Crystal nods. Her lips turn up into a huge smile flashing her dimples, and she leans in closer to gaze into this beautiful violet eyes.

"I promise not to tell a soul and I'll help you if I can."

He grins at her and leans in closer to whisper in her ear. He raises his left hand and slides his fingers through her hair to hold her neck. He pulls her towards him and leans in to whisper.

"What I'm going to tell you is important and please believe in me. I'm Samyaza and my friend is Apollyon. I need your help because I'm naked and I don't know where I am. I don't know how long he's going to take, but I can't stay here in my naked state."

Crystal nods and bites her lower lip, trying to control her reaction to his nearness. She swallows to push back the moan and to control her body.

"He went back into Hell."

He pulls back to gaze into her eyes to see her reaction.

"Hell?"

"Yes."

"That's hard to believe, Sam."

"I'm telling you the truth. It's good that you never entered because you wouldn't be able to leave."

Her color drains from her face and her eyes shine brightly searching his. She licks her lower lip and frowns.

"You're serious."

"Yes."

"Oh gosh, that's so hard to absorb and assimilate."

She trembles and closes her yes. *Hell? Omg! This is not supposed to be real? Or is it? Samyaza sounds so familiar.*

She opens her eyes and clasps her hands together, frowning. She blinks rapidly and looks quizzically at Sam.

"You're name is Samyaza?"

"Yes."

He looks at her, watching her eyes to gauge her reactions. He takes her hand in his and strokes her wrist, feeling her heart rate.

She bites her lower lip and then she licks it nervously.

"I read about Samyaza, a fallen angel. Were you named after him?"

Samyaza slowly smiles and leans in closer to her. He places a soft kiss on her pale cheek.

"Sweet Crystal, I am Samyaza."

He pulls back to watch her, not releasing her hand.

"What! Is that for real? Omg!

Apollyon turns around, clenching his huge hands into fists. He snarls at Lucifer, curling his full upper lip.

"I know that you're not going to try to take me out, Luc! I'm the most powerful of all!"

Luc grins and nods, crossing his arms and shrugging.

"Lyon, you were. But I don't feel your powers. Yes, I am because you have no right to release Samyaza! He's in my domain for eternal punishment. What the fuck are you thinking?"

Lyon's face turns red. He furiously walks down the tunnel to stand in front of Luc. He emits his black and red smoke, he squints his eyes, and roars.

"Fuck you!"

"Hell! I'm not going to back down, Lyon!"

"The hell you are! It's been written."

"I was informed of this?"

"Fuck, Luc! I have to return to Samyaza. He's weak and could die. You allowed him to go without nourishment for too long. He's not healing and I barely felt his energy."

Luc raises his right hand and runs his fingers through his silky black hair. He frowns and growls angrily.

"I was sure that he was ok!"

"I'm leaving because I have to take care of him!"

Luc shakes his head and shoves Lyon back onto his backside. He falls onto him and punches him in the face.

"What the fuck do you think I'm going to do? Allow you to release him? Fucking no way!"

Apollyon moves his long powerful legs and pushes up to push Luc off him.

"Fuck you, Luc!"

He pushes Luc off him, flips him over, and Luc slides down the ledge. Lyon approaches him, growling. Lyon's swirling gray-blue eyes glow. His fangs extend and his horns emerge. He's furious and ready to fight Lucifer.

Luc laughs and swings his arm back to throw a fire bolt at Lyon.

Lyon jumps up and away from the bolt. He advances towards Luc, growling.

Shasi instantly shifts into her dragon and flaps her wings. She shoves Luc of the ledge into the bottomless fire pit.

Luc roars, his eyes red sparks flash as he falls.

"Fuck, I'm going to help Samyaza. Shasi go and rescue Luc."

Shasi instantly turns back into her demon and shakes her head.

"Master, I don't need to rescue Luc because he's going to be ok. This is his domain."

Lyon frowns, and shrugs his huge shoulders. He runs down the tunnel towards the portal. He takes a step to exit but he bounces back.

"What the fuck!"

He tries again but the portal is closed.

"Fuck! I have to wait until tomorrow. Damn it. I hope that Samyaza is ok."

He punches the portal wall angrily. He turns to look down the tunnel at Shasi. He runs back towards her.

"Shasi, take me to my Citadel."

Shasi smiles and nods. She instantly shifts into her dragon.

Lyon jumps onto her back and holds on tight.

Six

William walks out of his office and down the hallway. The building is eerily silent especially after everyone has gone home, and the constant noise of the day has stopped.

He pulls at his tie and runs one hand through his soft, dirty blond hair. He looks out of the huge windows into the full moon, stopping in the middle of the hallway.

"What the fuck!"

I feel his pull, his wild hungry need. Damnit! He really is connected to me. He took my soul. What the fuck! I can't resist him even if I try. I know that he's all bad, sinfully addicting, and totally evil for the nation.

How can I stop him, save my soul in the process, and my heart? I can't love him!

The cell phone beeps and he pulls out his cell from his slacks. He looks down at the message from Carol.

Darling, I have dinner ready. I miss you. Love you

He grinds his molars and closes his eyes.

I can't break our engagement. We've been together for years and I proposed a few weeks ago. I can't and I won't. I have to be true to her and my principals.

The cell phone beeps again and he sighs. *I have to answer her because she won't stop until I tell her that I'm on my way. Damn it!*

William looks at his cell message.

My Pet, I'm waiting for you. I have dinner and some amazing wine. I need you!

Fucking hell! My damn cock is reacting to his summons. I can't believe this!

Carol sends other text with her picture. She's wearing a sexy black dress with fuck me heels

I'm all ready for you Babe.

He looks at her picture and doesn't feel a thing. He grinds his molars and quickly texts her.

Sorry, Carol, I'm finishing up some contracts. I'll be here all night.

He presses send button and walks out of the building into the parking garage. He pulls off his tie and suit jacket. He tosses them onto the passenger seat.

He slides into the driver's seat and adjusts his aching cock.

I can't fucking believe this wild hunger.

He slides his hand down his slacks and adjust his cock. He closes his eyes and thinks of Sorath. His cock twitches and weeps with the thought of Sorath.

Without thought he turns on the car and drives fast, down the coast to Sorath's home. He pulls into the circular driveway and stops at the door.

He opens his silver BMW and slides out, slamming the door. He's anxious to enter the house and fall into Sorath's arms.

He walks up the door and the door is opened by the butler. The butler nods at him, extending his arm and motioning for him to enter.

"This way. My Master is waiting for you."

William walks into the house and waits for the butler to close the door.

The butler walks past William and up the stairway to the second floor. He walks down the huge hallway to the end and knocks on the black wooden door.

"Enter."

Sorath waits for William in his room with the table set and the windows open. The fresh sea breeze enters into the room.

The huge full moon shines brightly, illuminating the coast. The waves appear to glitter with the moon's bright glow.

The butler opens the door and allows William to enter. William stops at the door and looks at Sorath, forgetting about everything else.

The butler steps out of the room and closes the door. Sorath smiles a small sexy smile and he waves his hand to lock the door. He gazes into William's heated green eyes.

"My Pet, you look sinfully delicious and I'm famished."

He extends his hand out for William to take it. William looks at Sorath and slowly walks towards him, gazing into his gleaming blue eyes. He looks at his full red lips and then down to his crotch.

Oh fuck, my mouth waters just thinking of tasting his cock again. What the hell!

William stops in front of him. He gazes into Sorath's hot hungry eyes, watching him lean in closer.

Sorath grabs Williams's shoulders and pulls him closer. He moves his right hand up to William's neck and holds him close for a hungry kiss. He takes his mouth sliding his velvety tongue into William's mouth. He sucks, and strokes his tongue. A dark deep growl starts from the center of Sorath's soul and erupts from his mouth.

William returns his kiss. He moves his arms around his waist, and slides his hands up Sorath's back.

Sorath slides his hands down to unbuckle William's pants, pulls down the zipper, and grasps his engorged, hot cock. His hand runs down the length, cups William's balls, and then runs back up to cup his weeping crown. He growls and rubs his hand all over, spreading his seed.

"Yes, sweet Pet. You're finally here. I've been thinking of you all day."

Sorath falls onto his knees and takes William's cock into his mouth to love.

William holds onto Sorath's head, throwing back his own head, groaning and shaking.

I should fight this insane passion. I should fight him, but I can't. His touch, his scent, and his cock drives me insane. I'm his whore.

Crystal looks out into the ocean from the entrance of the cave. She crosses her arms, and frowns. Her eyes roam the horizon for answers, moving side to side.

What should I do? I don't know him from Adam but, geeze, I feel him. I feel his honesty and also I feel his soul. I feel connected to him.

She then turns to look at Sam. She gazes deep into his beautiful violet eyes, searching for his brilliant soul. She nibble her lower lip, blushing. She places her hand on his shoulder.

"Samyaza, I can help you. I'll take you home. I'll give you some food and clothes. Then we can return to search for your friend, but I think that he won't be able to use the magical entrance."

Samyaza smiles a small sexy smile, nods, and leans in closer. The waves crash against the rocks, foaming and sweeping in closer to them.

"I really have no way of thanking you for helping me and trusting with your heart. I promise that I won't hurt you, Crystal."

He moves in closer and kisses her softly on her soft lips.

Yes, she's simply sweetness and passion. I feel her, I smell her intoxicating spicy scent, and her beautiful soul is engrained into mine. God almighty. She's mine! My soul mate!

Crystal sighs, closing her eyes. She moves her hand up his shoulder into his long silky wet hair. She opens her mouth to allow him to deepen his kiss.

Oh gosh, he's so freaking hot, incredibly delicious. He totally has my heart and soul in his hands. I can't believe how he makes me feel, and I can barely breathe.

His aura, his soul, affects my breathing. My heart feels like it's going to explode.

Samyaza takes possession of her mouth and explores every nook.

The sounds that she makes and her spicy scent drugs me. I want more but we need to leave.

He pulls back and gazes into her beautiful passionate bright hazel eyes.

"We need to leave, I'm weak and I'm losing energy fighting off this chill."

Crystal eyes widen, surprised and concerned, and she nods. She looks away and her eyes stop at his waist. *Oh yeah, he looks yummy.*

She bites her lip to keep the groan from escaping. She blushes a deep red and looks away, embarrassed.

"Oh yes, I'm sorry. I wasn't thinking."

Crystal raises her hand and pushes back her long hair from her flushed face.

Samyaza throws back his head and laughs a deep, throaty, sexy laugh. His strong neck muscles flex and his vein throbs with the beat of his heart. He then smiles down at her. He leans in closer, and takes her hand.

"Crystal, don't be embarrassed over something that is so natural because I plan on getting to know every single inch of your beautiful body."

He raises his other hand and slides it through her long, shiny black hair.

She blushes a deeper red, her upper lip trembles, and a light sprinkle of sweat on her skin glistens in the moonlight.

"Ok, I'm good with that. Let's get out of here. My car is parked in the parking lot."

"Ahhhhh,…car?" He frowns, his brows gather together, and he looks at her with a question in his eyes.

"Yeah, my car."

Crystal grins, and stands up along with Samyaza. She holds onto his hand as he sways from side to side, unbalanced.

"Oh geeze, I forgot how weak you are. Hold onto me and we can take it slow."

Samyaza nods. His color has drained from his face, and his eyes look dim. He follows her and they walk through the El Matador cave's entrance. They stop and Samyaza looks around.

"It appears that the portal has closed."

Crystal eyes widen and she nods.

"Is that what that is? A portal? To where?"

Samyaza looks down.

"It's the portal to Hell."

"You're serious? Omg, that's so freaking amazing! And so scary."

Samyaza slowly and weakly pulls her into his arms. He places both shaking hands on her shoulders. He gazes deeply into her excited eyes.

"Crystal, promise me that you won't ever attempt to enter the portal. Promise me that you won't tell a soul." Crystal closes her eyes and trembles. She opens her eyes and gazes into his. The glow is quickly fading.

Oh wow, he's getting weaker and he looks ill. I have to get him home and give him some of my chicken soup.

"Samyaza, I promise I won't ever tell a soul."

Shasi flies through Hell's stations and stops at the bottom of the abyss to the Citadel. She flaps her long wings and shrieks excitedly.

Apollyon slides off her back and stands looking around. He clenches his large hands into fists. He turns around fuming and his horns start to emerge from his temples. His swirling gray-blue eyes glow and he emits black and red florescent smoke.

"Shasi, I need you to get me inside my damn realm. I can't fucking believe this. I don't have enough powers to enter."

Shasi instantly transforms into her true form. Her long black hair swings back and forth below her firm ass.

She raises her arms, outstretched straight, and she places her right hand on top of her left hand and she bows her head.

"Master."

She then waves her hand and the huge silver embossed doors appear.

Lyon smiles and nods.

"Thanks Shasi, I can't wait to sleep in my bed after thousands of years. I don't want anyone to disturb my sleep."

"Yes, Master."

He walks down the black granite hallway. The black granite is shined to a mirror finish. The black candle's flames dance, illuminating the hallway.

He walks towards his bedroom, looks around to, and nods. His bedroom is huge, with the south wall made of crystal glass and looks out into the eternal waterfall. The northern wall has a huge crown made of silver and crystal hanging over the beautiful intricately embellished silver bed.

A pair of silver silk drapes are drawn back and tied, with a black ribbon that has silver edge, to the silver bed pillars. The bedspread is silver with a black embossed scroll pattern.

"Yes, it's like I left it. Nobody has been inside my Citadel."

He walks down the east side of his chambers and into a huge bathroom. The lights turn on instantly and the silver faucets shine brightly. The eight shower heads instantly turn on around the circle pool and he walks into the pool of steaming water. He sighs and sits on the first step. He leans back and closes his tired eyes.

A few moments later Shasi runs into his room, searching for him.

"Master!"

He shakes his head and ignores her.

"Master! Master! Lucifer is inside and refuses to leave! Please allow me to roast him."

Lucifer laughs and watches her enticing long hair sway back and forth over her firm round ass.

"Lyon, I need to talk to you! Keep your demon away from me!"

Lyon opens his beautiful swirling gray-blue eyes, frowning.

"Luc, stay away from Shasi!"

Luc stops at the door of the bath chamber. He leans against the wall, and grins. He crosses his left ankle across his right. His brilliant blue eyes glitter wickedly.

"Luc, what to do you want? I'm not going to fight you. I want you on my team."

"You think that you are going to get rid of me that easy? Not!"

Lyon turns his head to glare at him, his swirling gray-blue eyes glow, and he releases his red and black florescent smoke. He snarls at Luc. His red horns start to emerge from his temples and his upper lip curls into a snarl.

"Damn you, Luc! You're trying my patience! Pray for cover when I regain my full powers. Your ass is mine! You're a pansy next to me!"

Luc throws back his head, his chests trembles, and a deep chuckle echoes throughout the bath chamber. His even white teeth gleam, and he closes his eyes. His white shirt is open at the neck and his strong thick neck veins throb erratically.

Lyon sits up in the pool and closes his eyes, clenching his jaw. His wet black hair is clumped together in wet locks, and the water drips down the wide expanse of his back and chest. His skin is turning red, and he's turning into his true nature.

Luc stops laughing and nods at him. He uncrosses his legs and turns to place a hand on the wall. He narrows his beautiful eyes, shaking his head.

"The fucking problem here is that you came into my domain and released a very important guest. Samyaza has a sentence of eternal punishment."

Lyon stands from the pool and walks out onto the black shining granite, dripping water. He snaps his fingers to dress. He stops a few inches from Luc and leans in close to his face. He hisses and emits his red and black florescent smoke.

"Back off and listen. I did get the word to release the Watchers. I also need you on my team. The Dark Prince has come of age and is gaining power. I'm too weak to fight him now."

Luc raises his hands. He rests his huge hands on Lyon's chest, and shoves Lyon back. Lyon staggers back and regains his balance, snarling.

"Fuck!"

Luc walks away from Lyon a few steps, frowning. He abruptly turns around to glare at him.

"Why should I join your team? I'm not part of humanity Watchers. And damn it! I'm here because of the humankind. I don't see why I should join this alliance to save their selfish greedy asses!"

"Fuck you, Lucifer! I need you and the Watchers' powers to fight him. He's as powerful as I am. I need to terminate the Dark Prince and therefore I need all of your powers to help me destroy the Dark Prince!"

Luc grinds his jaw and snarls at him. "Not happening!"

Lyon clenches his huge hands into fists and frowns. He looks past Luc towards the wall in his bedroom and strides out of the bath chamber and into his bedroom.

He takes long strides towards the huge wall and stops to read the glowing glyphs. He crosses his arms and reads the glowing scripture on his wall.

Luc follows him looking around his bedroom.

"What's up?"

Lyon ignores him and reads the scripture to himself.

"Apollyon, my destroyer, your time hasn't arrived but I'm going to ask that you heed my bidding. The Dark Prince has arrived and is gaining power. His plan to rule humanity is absurd and I won't allow it. Humankind are my children and I won't allow him to dominate nor destroy humanity. You will gather the Watchers and unite your powers to conquer the Dark Prince."

"Lyon, where are you getting that from?"

Luc stares at the wall, frowning. He shakes his head and turns away.

"I'm leaving. I've had enough of this bullshit."

Lyon turns around and glares at him.

"Lucifer! I was reading the scripture on the wall. What the fuck! I need you!"

Luc stops and turns around, grinning. He nods at him.

"Well, let me think about it."

"Asshole!"

Luc shrugs and walks out of Lyon's bedchamber, towards the hallway to teleport out of the Citadel.

Crystal places her arm through Samyaza's left arm to help him walk over the wet rocks and the sand. The waves rush onto the beach in a fast erratic tempo, crashing over their feet.

"I'm going to take you home, Samyaza, and get you some food. Please lean on me, I know that you're still weak."

Sam nods, taking a deep breath to gather some strength. He moves his long muscular legs and grinds his jaw.

Damn it! I still have open wounds on my back, I can feel them. I wonder if Crystal will be horrified when she see the wounds. I hope that they're not too horrific.

They walk up the wooden stairs up to the parking lot. The night is dark, the crescent moon and the stars twinkle in the night, providing some light. The coastal highway is isolated.

Crystal walks up to the only car in the parking lot. She pulls out her remote key and opens the car. The doors unlock.

Samyaza narrows his eyes and his eyes roam over the silver Honda. His eyebrows gather together in a frown and he moves his head as he looks at the car. *What in god almighty is this? What unusual furniture.*

"Samyaza, this is my car."

Crystal gazes up at him. Her eyes widen, noticing his reaction to the car.

"Yeah? What does it do? This car is useful for what?"

Crystal purses her lips to control her amusement and reaches for the car's door. She pulls it open and nods to him.

"Sam, come over here and sit on this seat. I'm going to drive this car to my home. We will be there in a few moments."

Samyaza raises his eyebrows, but his eyes look inside the car. He turns to look at Crystal, shaking his head.

"This space looks small and I'm not sure that I will fit."

He crosses his arms and looks at Crystal's amusement. He narrows his eyes and focuses on her beautiful hazel eyes as they sparkle.

She moves her hands up to push her hair back from her eyes. She nods at him, grinning.

"Yazy, you will fit and you're going to enjoy the ride. Come on, slide onto the seat so we can go home. I know that you're weak and need food."

He frowns and looks back inside the car and shrugs. *Hell, I don't have a choice and I don't know what in the world this car will do but I'm going to trust my mate.*

He slides his long muscular left leg into the car and slides onto the seat. He then swings his right leg inside the car and wiggles to adjust his huge body in the small space.

He turns to look up at Crystal nodding. He pulls the leather coat to cover himself.

"I'm in and now what?"

Crystal throws back her head, laughing and shaking her head. She then looks down at him, grinning, and leans into the car. She reaches for the seatbelt, gazing into his beautiful violet eyes.

"Yazy, let me buckle you up and then I'm going to sit on the seat next to you. I know that you're going to enjoy the ride."

Samyaza raises his right black eyebrow and narrows his eyes. He watches her pull the seatbelt and insert it into the seatbelt buckle.

"Really?"

"Yeah."

Crystal smiles and moves back out of the car. She winks at him, steps back, and closes the car door. She walks around the car and opens the driver's door. She smiles and slides onto the seat. She inserts the key and turns on the car.

Samyaza hisses, his eyes widen, and he turns to look at her.

"That's very unusual noise. What is it?"

Crystal laughs a pleasingly soft sound and she grins. She moves her hand to place it on his shoulder. She gazes into his startled eyes.

"Yazy, this is a car and it runs with an engine. The engine makes this sound but don't worry. Just sit back and enjoy the ride."

He raises his eyebrow and his eyes glow brilliantly. He nods and leans back into the seat and crosses his arms.

"I'm going to follow your directions."

Crystal laughs and moves her hand to shift the car into reverse. She watches Samyaza move forward and back in the seat, not expecting the movement.

He glares at her and frowns.

"Sweet god almighty! Are you attempting to kill me?"

Crystal shakes her head and grins. She winks at him and takes his hand in hers.

"Yazy, please relax and trust me. We drive cars every day and everyone owns a car. I'll teach you to drive."

Samyaza nods and relaxes as much as he can. He looks out the window at the coast.

"The view is beautiful."

He turns to look at her profile. He squints his eyes to focus on every single feature.

"Sweet Crystal, you're incredibly beautiful. Tell me about you and your family."

Crystal glances quickly over at him and smiles.

"Yazy, I'm a twin. My sister name is also Crystal but she likes to be called Cryssi. My family lives in another state. I work as a Paramedic."

"Oh damn, you're a twin? I hope that you're not identical because I don't want any games. What in the world is a paramedic?"

"Yes, but no. She has blue eyes and I have hazel eyes. She's likes to color her hair with highlights and I don't. I'm sure that you'll be able to tell us apart. She also has a tattoo on her foot and I have one on my hip."

She glances quickly over at him, grinning.

"Ah, tattoo?"

"Yes Yazy, I'll show it to you later. I'm a paramedic. I help save people that are ill. I attend to them until we arrive at the hospital. The doctor then takes over. We give them the first medical attention that is crucial for their survival."

"Uh…hmm. So much to learn. Medical? Doctor? I'm not sure that I understand, Sweetness."

She smiles at him, and clutches his hand to assure him. She then returns her hand to the steering wheel.

"I'm going to show you and explain everything that is new to you."

"I imagine that would be a lot."

He moves his head on the headrest to look at her as she drives. His eyes moves down to her full firm breasts and suddenly he inhales deeply, shuddering. He moves his hand to his lap to control his cock's reaction to her. He closes his eyes to inhale deeply and exhales.

Damn it, my body is so turned on by her and her sweet scent. I have to control this because I don't want to scare her. She's pure and innocent. Oh god almighty! She's my mate.

He moves his hand to clasp hers, urgent to claim her in a small way.

Crystal glances quickly over at him, raising her right eyebrow.

"Yazy, are you ok? We're almost home."

Samyaza slowly smiles and opens his beautiful violet eyes, turning his head to look at her.

"Sweet Crystal, I'm well. I'm only hungry and weak but once I eat I should recover instantly."

"That's good to hear."

"This car is not bad at all. It's a lot better than a horse."

Crystal laughs, and turns to look ahead of the road. She pushes the gas pedal. The car lurches forward and races down the Southern California coast.

A few moments later she pulls off the highway and drives down the streets. She finally reaches her small condo. She pulls into her driveway and presses the button to open her garage door. She bites her lower lip and looks around.

Yeah, nobody is around. Sometimes I have a feeling that someone is watching me. I can't stand it but now Yazy is here.

She pull up into her garage and presses the button. She closes the garage door.

Samyaza is leaning forward, looking around to see everything that is new to him. He turns to glance at her, raising his right eyebrow.

"God almighty! So much to learn!"

Crystal laughs at him and nods. She raises her right hand and cups his left cheek. She smiles, gazing into his eyes.

"I'm sure that you're going to love all the technology and food. Now let's go into my home so I can feed you."

Samyaza nods, smiling at her.

"Sweetness, that sounds so delicious because I'm a starving man."

Sorath stands across the street in the shadows. He takes out a Djarum Black and lights up. He narrows his eyes, watching the garage door close.

"I'm going to take her and she's going to be a magnificent servant. I love it when my servants are pure and innocent. She's going to fit perfectly into my plans. Well, except for William, but he's different. He's totally mine."

He inhales deeply of the clove flavored cigarette. The black cigarette smoke shrouds him. He then takes out his phone to text William.

My pet, I'll be home in a few. I'm taking care of business.

He grins and takes another smoke of his cigarette, nodding.

Hell yes, I can't wait to return to his arms. I fucking can't resist William. Tomorrow I'm going to take her.

Seven

Crystal opens the car door, slides out, and closes the door. She walks quickly around the car and opens Samyaza's door, smiling down at him.

"Allow me to unbuckle the seatbelt. Yazy, we're home. I'm going to give you some chicken soup that I have in the refrigerator. I know that you're going to love it. While I warm up the soup, you can take a shower. I have some huge sweats that my father left when my parents were here a few months ago. You can use those. Oh yeah, he also left some jeans and t-shirt because they bought a lot of stuff at the outlets. He decided to leave a few items behind."

Samyaza watches her intently, listening to her chatter trying to understand what she's talking about. He closes his eyes.

"Oh wow, I don't have a clue what you're talking about, Sweetness. I only understand about the soup. What is a shower, a refrigerator, and sweats? Geeze!"

Crystal laughs, reaching for the seatbelt buckle. She then moves back to help him out of the car.

"You'll see in a few minutes. I'm going to take you to my bedroom and you take a shower while I get the soup ready for you. You'll be relaxing in no time."

She steps back and extends her hand to help him out of the car. Samyaza takes her hand and slides out.

He moves away from the car and she closes the door.

She turns and slides her arm into his left arm. She walks towards the garage door that leads into the small kitchen.

"Yazy, come inside and I'll show you."

He nods and follows her lead. His eyes move rapidly, taking everything in. He looks at the new and different building structure, the items in the kitchen, and appliances. He raises his eyebrows.

"Yes, I see that I have a lot to learn. Some things are slightly different from what I left behind."

He looks down at her smiling. His stomach growls and he grins.

"Come on, you can investigate later. I'm taking you to my bedroom and into the shower. I know that you're going to love it!"

Samyaza nods and follows her into the small living room and down the hallway.

She walks into her bedroom. She crosses the room and walks into the bathroom, turning on the light. She turns around to look at him and winks. She slides the shower door open and leans in to turn on the shower.

"Ok, Yazy, take off that jacket and walk into the shower stall. The water should be nice and warm. You'll love it!"

Samyaza raises his eyebrows, looking at the water spraying from the shower head. He looks at the steam swirling around.

"Ah…yeah."

He shrugs his shoulders and the jacket falls off his shoulders and slides down his wounds. He winces and closes his eyes. He takes in a sharp breath.

"What's wrong?"

Crystal quickly steps around him to look at his back. She gasps, outraged, and her color drains from her face.

"Omg! What did they do to you! Your flesh is totally shredded. How in the world have you been able to tolerate the pain?"

Samyaza clenches his jaw and turns to around to look at her. He narrows his eyes and nods.

"Sweet Crystal, I'll be much better as soon as I eat a meal. I would heal quicker if I have more blood."

He watches her closely, watching her pale complexion.

"Yazy, are you serious! Look at your back!"

She points to the mirror, frowning, and turns him around.

Samyaza turns around and looks into the large bathroom mirror. He frowns, and nods. He closes his eyes.

Yes, that's what flogging does to you but I'll be ok. I understand why she's so upset. I need to convince her that I'm going to be ok.

He opens his eyes and gazes into her eyes. He raises both hands and rests them on her trembling shoulders.

"Sweet Crystal, please believe in what I'm going to tell you. Remember that I'm an angel. Well, a fallen angel, and most important immortal. That means that I usually regenerate but I was without sustenance for such a long time that my energy is depleted. I need nourishment or blood to boost my energy. My body will regenerate soon as I have the power that I need."

He looks deeply into her beautiful hazel eyes, reaching her soul.

She blinks rapidly and her tears fall down her face. She shakes her head, trying to understand what he told her.

"Yazy, I don't understand how someone could hurt you so. It's too painful to see. I hurt for you."

Her tears continue to fall down her face and he pulls her into his arms.

"My sweet Crystal, please don't shed your tears for me. I don't deserve your tears. I promise you that I'm going to be ok."

She buries her face into his sculpted chest. She rests her hands on his waist, sobbing. A few seconds later she pulls back to look up at him and blinks rapidly.

"Yazy, take more of my blood. I don't mind. Please."

Samyaza raises his black eyebrow and his violet eyes glow.

"Sweetness, are you sure? I don't want to hurt or scare you."

Crystal nods and bites her lower lip. She moves her hands up to his shoulders and raises up onto her tip toes. She slides her hands up his neck and pulls him down. She gazes deeply into his eyes.

"Yazy, I feel your soul, and my heart beats with yours. I know that you wouldn't ever hurt me. Please take the blood that you need to heal."

She kisses him softly, moaning into his mouth. He takes her mouth in a deep hungry kiss. He devours her mouth and slowly enjoys her tastes.

Yes, she's mine and I'm hers. Our heart and souls are one.

Yazy opens his eyes and watches her through the mirror. He moves his mouth away from hers and kisses her jaw down to her neck. He licks and places his lips on her throbbing jugular vein. He bites her and draws her rich red blood, closing his eyes and groaning.

"Ahhhh......Yazy."

Crystal shudders and melts right into him. She slides her arms round his waist, avoiding his wounds.

Yazy drinks from her until he feels his energy increase. He watches his wounds start to heal. He sees her start to lose her coloring and pulls back quickly, licking the bite wounds. He holds onto her shoulders to keep her from swaying.

"Sweetness, are you okay?"

His beautiful glowing violet eyes roam all over her face to verify her state.

Crystal nods and gazes up at him. She starts to slide down and he picks her up into his arms. He turns around and walks out of the bathroom. He walks over to the bed and places her onto the dusty rose bedspread.

Crystal closes her yes and sighs. She holds onto his neck, pulling him down next to her.

"Yazy, stay with me for a few minutes. I'm feeling better."

Samyaza nods and falls down onto the bed next to her. He pulls her into his arms and holds her close.

"Sweetness, please tell me that you're feeling better. I'm never ever going to take blood from you. I almost drained you."

He kisses her face and then her lips, holding her tight.

Crystal wraps her arms around his neck and returns his hungry kiss.

A few moments later Yazy pulls back and smiles down at her. He rests his forehead against hers, shaking.

"Sweetness, I'm hungry and I'm going to take that shower that you promised me."

Crystal grins and nods, releasing his neck. She laughs and blushes.

"Yazy, take that shower. I hope that the water is still warm."

Samyaza grins. Nodding he turns to slide off the bed. His back is completely healed.

"Omg Yazy! Your back is healed. I don't see one single wound!"

Crystal scoots across the bed to reach him. She runs her hand all over his smooth back. She nods and looks at him, smiling.

"I'm so happy that you can heal like that. I was very scared and worried."

Samyaza smiles and leans in to kiss her small cute nose.

"Don't ever worry about me because I am immortal. I will always regenerate and I'm the one that will take care of you."

Crystal blushes and nods. She slides off the bed and takes his hand.

"You take your shower and I'll heat up your soup."

He laughs a deep throaty sound and nods. He stands and follows her back into the bathroom. He gives her a quick kiss on her soft swollen lips and walks into the shower stall.

Crystal reaches over to close the shower door and walks out of the bathroom.

"I'll be waiting for you."

Oh fuck, I have the hardest time resisting her charms. I have to wait because I don't want to love her until she's really ready and sure. I know that she's mine but does she? I feel her desire but I want to have her love.

He reaches for the white Dove soap and smiles as he smells it. He nods and closes his eyes as he slides the soap all over his body.

This shower reminds me of the warm spring water falls that I enjoyed when I was last on the earth realm. I can't wait to start my life with Crystal because I know that I'm not going to let her go.

Lyon walks around his room, running his hands through his long hair. He releases his black and red smoke and his red horns start to emerge.

Oh damn it! I haven't changed into my true form since before I left my realm. I need to give into my body needs and enjoy a slight respite.

He allows his body to change into his true form. The red horns emerge to their full size and his skin changes into a darker, golden-red tone.

I hope that Samyaza is ok because I left him on the earth realm without any type of money, clothing, or even an idea of where to go. Damn it!

He paces around his room and stops at the huge glass wall. He looks into the garden and at the crystal clear waterfall. He smiles and leans forward placing his hands on the glass.

I had forgotten how beautiful my realm is and how much I missed it.

Shasi walks down the hall and stops at Apollyon's bedroom door. She taps on it and waits.

Lyon pulls away from the glass wall and turns to look at the door.

"Yeah!"

Shasi opens the door and walks into the room. She stops at the center of the room. Her long black hair swings back and forth below her firm ass.

She raises her arms, outstretched straight, and she places her right hand on top of her left hand and she bows her head.

"Master, is there anything that you require?"

"No, Shasi. I'm going to bed because I plan on leaving tomorrow. I need to search for Samyaza on the earth realm."

Shasi raises her head and nods. She crosses her arms below her firm breasts and smiles.

"Master, you could search for Samyaza on your crystal sphere in your throne room. I'm sure that you will see if he's ok and where he is. He does have his powers, unlike you."

Lyon hisses angrily and then slowly forces a smile. *Damn it! It's not her fault that my powers are bound. Yeah, I'll should be able to locate Samyaza and it would be a lot easier to see where I can locate him on the earth realm.* He nods, and smiles at her.

"Thank you, Shasi, for reminding me of my sphere."

Shasi nods and waits for him to dismiss her.

"You can take your rest."

"Yes, Master."

She bows her head and turns to walk out of his room.

Lyon sighs with relief and turns to walk towards his huge bed. He grins and falls onto it, falling to sleep instantly.

Crystal smiles as she pushes the microwave button to heat up a bowl of chicken soup. She turns around and walks out of the kitchen and down the hallway towards her bedroom. She looks through the bathroom door, nodding.

Samyaza turns the knobs. He raises one eyebrow, nodding. *Ok, this is really easy.*

He turns to his left and slides the shower door open. He looks right into Crystal's eyes. His lips turn up into a sexy smile and his beautiful violet eyes glow. He looks healthy, young and hot.

"Yazy, the towel is on the wall. I'm getting you some clothes to wear."

He nods, extends his sinewy arm and grabs the towel.

"Ok, it smells delicious."

Crystal laughs and walks over to her lovely maple dresser and pulls out the bottom drawer. She gazes into the mirror as she reaches down.

Oh…I feel so different but I look the same. I don't know what it is but I feel that everything is different now. I feel disconnected from the world, like I'm in another world but yet I'm not. It's such an odd feeling. I can't believe it! I have a real angel in my home. Oh wow, this is surreal, and I must be crazy.

She looks down at the folded black sweats and t-shirt. She grabs them and turns to look at Samyaza enter the room with the towel wrapped around his waist.

He stops in front of her and places his hands on her shoulders, gazing into her beautiful hazel eyes. Their eyes connect, their souls merge, and their hearts beat as one.

"Sweetness, that was an amazing experience. I do feel a lot better. Thank you."

Crystal blushes, her eyes shine brightly, and her soft cheeks flush a soft rose. She smiles up at him.

"Yazy, I'm so happy that you look and feel better. I have your soup all warmed up and here's the sweats for you to wear."

She hands him the sweats and t-shirt.

"Thank you, Sweetness."

"You're welcome. I'll wait for you in the kitchen."

She turns to walk across the room and into the hallway. She walks into the kitchen and pulls open the microwave. She takes the bowl of soup out and turns to place it on the table, smiling.

Samyaza walks into the kitchen, looking roguish. He stands at the door until Crystal turns around.

Crystal laughs at him, shaking her head. "Oh my, I thought that they would fit you but I was wrong. They're a little tight and short."

Her eyes roam all over his amazing muscular body blushing. She looks at the tight black sweats constricting his aroused cock and the crown peeking out of the waistband.

Her eyes widen and she licks her lower lip. Then she bites her lip hard to control the soft moan. Her face flushes a deep red. Her feverish eyes glance up and their eyes lock. Her eyes widen, amazed at registering his passion. His beautiful violet eyes gleam.

Oh yes, he's beautiful and ah...so turned on. I can't believe it. He wants me? Geeze, he looks so yummy.

She raises her hand up to push her hair away from her flushed face and tucks it behind her ear.

"Uh…Yazy, your soup is ready."

"Ah…yes,… that smells good."

He runs his hands through his wet silky-black hair. He winks at her, takes a step closer to her, and slides his hand into her hair. He growls into her mouth right before he kisses her. He grasps her head and pulls her closer to kiss her deeply. He holds onto her head to keep it tilted at a certain angle to devour her mouth.

Crystal trembles and leans into him, melting against his hard body. She slides her arms around his waist and slides her hands up his back under the tight short black t-shirt.

Yes, his skin feels smooth and hot. I love how he makes me feel so beautiful and sexy.

Samyaza pulls back, grinning. His eyes roam all over her face, searching for her feelings.

"Sweetness?"

"Yes. Oh, yes."

He groans, pulling her back into his arms. He takes her mouth, submerging his tongue inside her mouth and stroking hers. He sucks and nibbles her full swollen lips, relishing her taste. He moves his mouth along her soft skin, enjoying her texture.

"Sweetness, I'm going to love you now and forever."

"Promise?"

Samyaza growls against her soft hot skin and nods. His response vibrates against her skin.

"Yes."

He takes soft nibbles along her long neck and sucks the soft sensitive curve of her neck and shoulder.

"I'm drunk on your taste and scent. Sweetness, I'm completely under your spell. I'm aching for your love."

Crystal moans softly against his chest, holding on tight. She trembles and pulls back to gaze into his passionate eyes.

"Uh…this is my first time."

She bites her lower lip, blushing deeply, gazing up into his eyes. Her eyes widen. She's nervous, and wary of his reaction.

Samyaza nods, narrowing his eyes and slowly smiles a small sexy smile. He whispers against her lips before he takes a kiss again.

"Sweetness, I know and I'll be very careful not to hurt you."

"Ahh…..hmm."

Crystal moans softly, falling apart under the wave of hot searing passion and love that runs through the blood throughout her body.

She slides her hands down his back and moves her right hand towards the front to slide it down inside the sweat pants. She moans, melting into him as she runs her hand down his hard hot cock.

He roars and pulls her closer, biting her shoulder and shuddering passionately. His body erupts into a hot inferno and he pulls back to gaze into her passionate eyes.

Samyaza holds onto her with his huge hands at her waist. He looks at her swollen lips and then his eyes move down to look at her swollen breasts. He narrows his eyes as he looks at her tight hard nipples protruding from the material.

He moves his hands and pulls her top up and over her head. He looks at her firm huge globes and at her sweet tight red nipples.

"Sweetness, you're pure heaven."

He leans down to take a tight nipple into his hot wet mouth and swirls his velvety tongue round the nipple, groaning he takes a bite.

Crystal moves her hands to rest on his shoulders holding on tightly, moaning and breathing deeply. Her body shakes uncontrollably.

"Arggg…..that feels so good, Yazy."

He moves his hot lips to her other breast and nibbles around her nipple, before taking a huge bite.

"I love your breasts, and your sweet nipples drug me."

He pulls her up into his arms and walks down the room and into the bedroom. He falls onto the bed and waves his hand to remove the remaining clothes.

"Oh, wow!"

Crystal opens her eyes and gazes into his gleaming violet eyes. She runs her hands down his engorged cock and looks down.

"Oh, my!"

She runs her fingers around his wide deep burgundy crown. She whimpers and bites her lower lip, closing her eyes.

"Sweetness I need you to look at me. I want to see your passion."

Crystal opens her feverish hazel eyes and nods. She smiles at him and moves her hand down his cock to cup his huge balls.

"Yazy, you're cock feels so yummy. I want to taste you so badly."

Samyaza growls and leans back onto his back, nodding. His cock springs forward, anxious for her touch.

"Oh, geeze, I don't know where to start."

Her soft breath blows on his crown right before she takes his crown into her hot wet mouth.

"Sweetness, easy. I'm going to explode!"

He growls, grasping the bedspread with his huge hands and his hips leaping up from the bed.

Yes! Oh yes! He tastes delicious. I can't believe how much I love his cock.

She runs her lips and tongue down the length of his cock, moaning. She trembles and looks up into his passionate eyes as she sucks his tight balls.

He throws back his head and his thick neck muscles flex and his veins throb. His long hair fans out on the bed.

Crystal moves her mouth up his cock and stops to trace his throbbing thick veins with the tip of her hot, wet tongue. Then she moves her mouth up to take his weeping crown into her mouth, moaning and closing her eyes.

Yeah, totally delicious cock and all mine. I know that he is.

"Sweetness, I need you. I need to taste you."

He opens his eyes to watch her suck his cock. He moves his hands to her head and runs his hands through her hair.

"That's it, Sweetness. Take my cock into your sweet mouth."

Crystal gazes into his passionate eyes. She sucks his crown softly, and shudders.

"Yazy, I'm burning up." She pulls away to look at his huge cock. She moans and runs her hand up and down his cock, trembling.

"Come here."

He runs his hand down to her pussy and spreads her flesh for his tongue. He moves down. He runs his tongue around her honey coated flesh, and takes her swollen flesh into his mouth.

"Oh, wow!"

Crystal pants and shudders, erupting into millions of searing tingles.

Fuck! Crystal is pure, innocent, and incredibly sweet. She tastes incredible, my blood is burning, and I'm so damn hard. I'm aching for her like I've never ached for a woman. She's burning her essence into my soul. Is it possible that she's my true mate? Dare I mate again?

I'm going to take some of her blood to gain some power but also to taste her again. Her rich spicy scent is driving me crazy.

He pushes her onto her back on the bed. He takes her lips with his teeth, slowly nipping and sucking her sweet blood.

Crystal moans and shifts, wrapping her arms around his neck. She pulls him closer to her, cradling him between her legs.

Oh yes! His cock feels so hard and yummy. I'm so hot and I need him. I can't believe how he turns me on. His taste is amazing and I feel connected to him.

He moves his lips down her jaw and buries his face in the curve of her neck. He kisses and sucks her skin right before biting her. He bites her deep enough to draw blood. He sucks her blood and his hips shift against her aching pussy.

Oh yes, I'm going to mark her as I take more blood. I feel so much better and she's my mate. I feel her soul embedded deep into mine.

He moves his hand up her thigh then stops at her ribs. He then slides his hand up to cup her huge breast and rubs his thumb over her tight, swollen nipple.

Crystal moans and shifts her hips to feel his cock against her aching pussy.

He draws more blood and then pulls away, licking the bite. He moves down her neck to her beautiful full breast.

"Crystal, I'm so hungry!"

He licks and sucks his way down to her breast and takes her tight nipple into his hot mouth. He rolls her nipple with his tongue and then bites around the areola, sucking more blood.

Damn, her taste is driving me insane and I love her breast, her spicy blood, and I'm so hungry. I want to love her.

"Ohhhhh……Yazy! Hmmm…I need you!"

She moves her right hand, sliding it down to grasp his hard cock. She runs her hand down his cock and then traces the wide crown.

"Yazy…huh……hmmm……your cock feels so yummy."

She moans, rubbing her pussy against his cock.

Samyaza is out of control, his skin is flushed, and his lips are red. Her blood has provided rich fuel for his body.

He growls and moves over to her other breast to torment her sweet nipple. He licks and sucks in between the valley of her breasts and looks up into her eyes.

"Crystal, are you sure?"

He moves his hand down to her hot, wet pussy. He slides his finger inside her pussy, watching her come undone.

Her hips leap up and she closes her eyes, moaning.

Samyaza's fingers slowly spread her pussy and rub her swollen flesh, growling as he does it. He buries his face between her breasts and then turns to take her tight nipple. He sucks and bites her.

"Omg, Yazy! I need you!"

My entire body is on fire and my pussy is aching for his cock.

Samyaza rubs his fingers around her swollen flesh. He slides his finger inside her hot wet pussy, gazing into her wild passionate eyes.

"Crystal, you're mine now and forever."

Crystal's feverish hazel eyes widen and she bites her lip. Her cheeks are flushed and her red lips are swollen. She nods and shifts her hips.

"Yes, forever!"

He shoves his throbbing cock inside her tight hot pussy.

He stops to look at her. His beautiful eyes gaze into hers, and waits for her ok.

"Crystal?"

She nods, her eyes watery, and smiles.

"Yes!"

He nods, he pulls out and plunges deep inside her tight pussy. He yells out, throwing back his head. The veins on his neck throb wildly, and his heart pounds.

"Crystal!"

He yells and then falls forward, pounding into her. His cock reaches deep inside, stretching her pussy.

"Omg! You feel so mouthwatering delicious!"

She shifts her hips to take his cock deeper inside, whimpering.

He moves his hands to her hips and pulls up her hips to slide in and out at a slower pace to watch his cock fuck her.

"Sweet Crystal, I love your pussy. It's so hot and tight. Your taste and your pussy drive me insane. You're deeply ingrained into my soul and blood. I'll never get enough of you."

He snarls and watches his big cock fuck her tight pussy. He pulls out and rubs his crown on her swollen flesh.

"Oh, yes! That feels so good, Samyaza."

He looks up, and nods. *Yeah, she recognizes that it's me.*

"You know that I'm Samyaza, the fallen angel?"

Crystal eyes widen, she blinks, and then nods. "Yes, I know that you are because I can feel your soul. I can see where you came from."

"I'm not an angel anymore. I'm a man and a starving man!"

She nods and smiles. "I feel you and I'm here for you. Always."

He growls and pulls his cock out of her pussy and leans down to take her swollen flesh into his mouth. He sucks and licks her honey.

"Gosh, you're drive me insane! I never dreamed that making love would be this incredible. My entire body is on fire. I love your mouth on my pussy. A delicious fire runs through my blood and my pussy aches!"

Yes, this is the sweetest blood ever. I love her and she's mine.

He sucks her sweet honey and slides his tongue into her pussy. He growls against her pussy and pulls back to fuck her.

He leans down and kisses her deeply as he fucks her long and hard. He releases her mouth and kisses his way down her jaw to mark her neck.

"Samyaza!"

"Crystal!"

They yell as one soul.

The next day the sun shines brightly through the soft sheer rose panels. Samyaza is completely naked on the bed and Crystal is on top of him, sleeping.

Yazy opens one eye and he looks at her sweet face. He grins, watching her soft swollen lips move as she talks in her sleep.

"Yazy."

She sighs and shifts slightly on his hips and takes his swollen cock into her pussy. She opens her eyes and pushes up with her hands on his chest.

She smiles and adjusts her hips to take him deep inside her tight pussy. Her breasts swell and her nipples look like sweet raspberries.

Yazy raises up onto his elbows and takes one sweet nipple into his mouth. He sucks her nipple and bites it, watching her passion flare up.

He turns to the other nipple, licks around the nipple and then sucks it inside his hot mouth.

She moves her hips to take his cock out. She rubs his engorged hot crown on her swollen flesh and whimpers. She bites her lower lip and closes her eyes, enjoying his cock.

"Ohhh….Yazy. My mouth waters, your cock feels so good."

She moans and whimpers in the early morning. She slowly takes his hard cock back inside, stretching her pussy walls, and she moans. She enjoys fucking him slow, savoring the burn and stretch, and the sweet rapture of his cock.

Samyaza eyes are half closed and he watches her face, which shows her ecstasy. He slowly grins and turns her over onto her back.

He takes her hands in his and moves his cock in and out in a fast pounding pace.

"Oh, yes! I love this way too."

He grins and fucks her fast and they reach their release as one soul. He falls onto his side and pulls her with him still connected. He closes his eyes and holds her tight.

"My sweet Crystal, I'm hungry."

Crystal opens her eyes and pulls back, grinning. Her hazel eyes sparkle and she nods.

Ok Yazy, I'll make some breakfast. Let's take a shower."

Samyaza grins and then laughs a deep throaty sound.

Sorath walks down the grayish-blue tiled hallway in his office and looks out into the ocean. He nods and turns to look at his assistant, also his disciple.

"Ms. Wells, I need you to prepare the invitations to my election dinner party for this weekend. I want to go over my agenda for my campaign because I want everyone out there pimping me."

"Yes, Master."

Sorath raises his eyebrow, glaring darkly at her. He shakes his head. He snarls at her, his bright blue eyes glow, and he walks over to her. He stands right in front of her, an inch away from her face. He clenches his jaw and snarls.

"I'm Senator Santanel when we're in the office."

Karen's complexion turns white and her glazed, dark brown eyes widen.

"Yes, Senator Santanel. It will never happen again. I have a list for you to review. The Senators are ready to raise the funds for the nationwide campaign."

Sorath grins. His blue eyes gleam brightly, and he nods. He rests his hands on his waist and raises his right eyebrow.

"I'm going to be in my office for a few hours. Make sure to get everything ready for my approval. I don't have time to waste. You know damn well that I'm on a tight schedule."

He narrows his eyes, nods and quickly turns on his heel and walks away. He takes long strides, pounding his huge black leather shoes into the tiled floor. He runs one hand through his shiny black hair. He walks into his office and shakes his head, gazing into the sun.

I'll be damned! It's my birthday and I feel my sire. I know that he's waiting for me to rule my dominion. I hate my birthday because I also think of my mother, the woman that gave birth to me, and tried to kill me. My guardian killed her and raised me. I hate the thought that my mother wanted me dead.

He walks over to the small bar and grabs a crystal glass. He takes the brandy crystal decanter and pulls the round top off. He pours the dark golden liquid into the glass. He places the decanter on the table and takes a drink of the brandy, closing his eyes. The fiery liquid burns down his throat.

He opens his eyes and takes a few steps towards the window to look out into the ocean.

"It's time for me to procure that sweet young girl from the beach. She's going to be my special sacrificial virgin, because I need her pure clean soul to increase my power. She's perfect, because she's pure and innocent. Yes, I know where she works and lives."

Sorath abruptly turns away from the glass window and walks back to the bar. He smiles, relaxed and optimistic with his plans.

His sets the crystal glass on the table and pulls out his cell phone. He moves his thumb over the screen and reads his new text messages, nodding.

"Fuck, yes! My Pet is going to meet me for dinner. I want William to help me with the girl."

Shasi walks down the hall and into the throne room, looking over at Lyon. Lyon is leaning against the marble table, staring into the crystal sphere and frowning.

"What the fuck! That bastard Sorath is pure evil! I can't believe that his sire is Asmodeus! Asmodeus is a vicious archdevil. He's the God-fiend of lust. Damn fiend loves to use trickery, he preys on the weak, and devours the innocent. He demands complete obedience from his disciples. Fuck, he seduced the young innocent girl and kept her chained to his bed until she conceived his spawn! Now I understand who and what Sorath Santanel is! Damn! He's the Dark Prince!"

Lyon stares into Sorath's glowing blue eyes and watches him take a drink of brandy. He clenches his hands into tight fists and grinds his molars.

"Damn it! I can't stop him alone. I now understand why I'm going to have to release the angels. Only our combined powers would be enough to stop him!"

She raises her hands up and nods her head forward. She then relaxes her stance and takes another step forward.

"Master! What do you see?"

Shasi walks up to him, frowning, and looks over his shoulders to see.

She nibbles at the right lower corner of her lip looking at the images in the sphere.

"Master, who's that? I can feel his evil soul."

She trembles and closes her eyes, shaking her head. She opens her eyes and looks over his shoulder again, shaking.

"Shasi, that's the Dark Prince and I need to stop him. I'm trying to locate Samyaza."

He sighs, squinting his eyes. He waves his hand over the sphere to see if it gives him Samyaza.

The ocean wave's splash over the rocks and the sun is low in the horizon and it's almost sunset. This is the image that appears in the sphere.

Lyon grins, and nods at Shasi.

"There he is, in the cave! Damn! He has a woman with him! Is he fucking crazy? Damn it!"

Shasi looks over his shoulders to look at Samyaza and the woman. She nods her head and slowly smiles.

"Master, that's his mate."

Lyon turns around to look at her, frowning. She shakes his head, clenching his hands into tight fists.

"That can't be possible, Shasi! He's a fallen angel!"

Shasi's eyes widen and she glances quickly at the sphere and sees Samyaza kiss Crystal. She nods her head quickly and points to the sphere.

"Master, they are mates. I can feel it and see it."

Lyon turns to look into the sphere, leaning in. He sighs and straightens up, moving his right hand through his long hair.

"What the fuck! I wasn't expecting this. I had no idea that we could mate. Damn it! I have to leave now because it's going to be twilight. Shasi, take me to the first station, to the portal."

Shasi nods, and chews her lip. She closes her eyes, inhales deeply, and then stares at him.

"Master, I want to go with you into the earth realm. I can help you."

Lyon turns to look at her, raising his right eyebrow and shaking his head.

"I don't want you to go, Shasi, because you can't shapeshift on earth. I don't want to babysit you when I need to focus on releasing the fallen angels."

Shasi stands straight and looks him in the eye. She speaks to him, firmly, in a low voice.

"Master, I can assist you in releasing the fallen angels. I can help you more on earth, much more than if I stay at the Citadel. Please reconsider."

Lyon frowns, his jaw muscle flexes from the pressure and he glances into the sphere. He squints his eyes and finally turns around to glare at her, nodding.

"Ok, I'll allow you to accompany me, but on one condition. You will obey my every order! I will order you to return to the citadel if you call any attention to yourself or the angels."

The red sparkles in Shasi's brown eyes glow and she nods her head.

"Yes, Master. I will only shapeshift if you request it."

Lyon nods and raises his hand to run through his black long hair.

"Right. Ok, let's go because it's almost time for the portal to open. Samyaza is waiting for me! That fucking ass is messing up! A mate? What the fuck is he thinking?"

"Yes, Master!"

Shasi follows him, taking long strides to keep up with him as they walk down the shiny granite hallway.

Apollyon walks to the huge titanium doors to enter into his gardens. He looks around, frowning, trying to remember, and frustrated, shakes his head. His eyes roam all over the gardens and looks up at the dark purple sky with two blood red moons illuminating his garden. He looks at the eternal waterfall and at the turquoise water falling and running off into a stream. Beautiful pink-turquoise butterflies hover over the different flowers on the ground.

He inhales deeply and exhales slowly, narrowing his eyes. His eyebrows gather together in an intense line, and he grinds his molars.

I can't fucking believe that I don't remember this and yet I remember other details of my Citadel. I can't wait to regain my powers and memories. .

"Master, we need to leave now!"

Lyon turns to look at Shasi, nodding at her. He watches her remove her clothes, instantly shifting into her favorite dragon and shrieks at him, the red specks in her huge eyes flashing eagerly. She flaps her huge wings and waits for him to climb onto her back.

"Shasi, let's go! We need to hurry."

Shasi shrieks loudly, flapping her huge wings. She spreads her wings and flies into the parallel dimension, Hell.

She flies up into tunnels, and around the fire pit, stopping at the top station of Hell. She waits for Lyon to jump off and breathes a bolt of fire striking the Furies on the wall at the entrance of the portal.

Lyon rests his hands, grinning. His lips turn up and his white even teeth gleam.

"Oh yeah, I love it!"

Shasi instantly shifts into her true form. She crosses her arms and waits for him, smiling smugly.

"Ok, we need to leave now!"

He takes long strides, his huge feet landing hard and loud on the limestone floor. He stops at the end of the tunnel, extending his right hand to place it at the gray limestone wall. He touches the limestone, waiting for the portal to open.

Shasi stands right behind him, her huge eyes sparkling as she watches him. She turns to look behind her for Furies. She smiles and waves at them at the opposite end of the tunnel.

The furies bounce around the walls and floor, moving their heads in a constant chatter.

"Fuck!"

Lyon's hand sinks into the limestone wall as the portal opens up. He grins and turns to look at Shasi.

"Follow me, Shasi. Remember you can't shift, eat humans, and kill."

"Yes, Master."

Shasi smiles, and when she nods her long ponytail swings across her ass.

Lyon walks through the portal and Shasi follows him.

Crystal laughs up at Samyaza, enjoying his reactions to the world. She takes a small lick of her ice cream. She extends her arm and offers it to him to taste.

Samyaza raises his eyebrow, looking at the ice cream. "Sweetness, what is that?"

Crystal laughs. The musical sound of her laughter fills Samyaza's soul with light and hope.

He leans in and takes a small nibble, nodding. "Yes, it does taste sweet and like strawberries but you're a lot better."

He grins and leans over to take a sweet kiss. He pulls her closer into his side. He pulls back, laughing.

"I would like to take you to the theatre. I'm sure that you'll enjoy it and you will be able to see how different it is."

Samyaza raises his hand and pushes her hair back. "Sweetness, I love your hair, and I love this new world but I especially love you."

Crystal's eyes shine happily and nods. "I like having you in my world, Samyaza."

"I'm ready to go and learn all about this theatre. I'm enjoying our time out."

"Yazy, I'm having a lot of fun. I'm so happy to have these days off work."

"Yeah, I'm going to locate my coins because I don't want you to work so hard. I want to spend our time together, enjoying our life."

Crystal laughs and nods, leaning in for another kiss. She pulls back and takes another lick of her ice cream.

"Thank you for looking out for me. I would love to spend all of my time enjoying you!"

"Right."

"Right."

She grins at him. She stands and pulls him up. They walk down the mall towards the theater.

A few hours later they exit the theater and Samyaza's eyes glow. He looks down at her and smiles.

"I did enjoy your theater and I can say that the world has evolved tremendously since I've been here."

"Oh Yazy, you sound so funny! I'm happy that you enjoyed it. Omg, it's time to go to the cave."

A few hours later, they arrive at the beach. Crystal and Samyaza smile at each other, holding hands as they walk down the wooden stairs towards El Matador cave to wait for twilight.

"Sweetness, I'm excited about our future together. I can't wait for you to meet Lyon. He's an awesome friend."

Crystal's face is flushed. Her eyes shine brightly, excited and anxious. She moves her left hand up to move a strand of hair from her lips. She smiles up at him, gazing deeply into his beautiful violet eyes.

"Yazy, I'm thrilled and so scared. I'm afraid that this is a dream."

Samyaza stops and pulls her into his arms, grinning. He leans down to kiss her upturned nose.

"I'm not going anywhere without you, Crystal."

"Ahhh….yes! I like that."

She smiles up at him, nodding. She stretches onto her toes to kiss his lips.

Crystal laughs and releases his hand to run across the beach towards the waves. She turns around and watches him chase her. She turns again and runs towards the cave entrance.

Eight

The evening is beautiful, a few clouds float around the moon, and the beach is calm. The waves crash onto the beach, foaming into bubbles.

Sorath walks down the stairs on the side of the cliff on his property. He stops at the last step, gazing out into the ocean, shoving his right hand into his black wool pants pocket. He pulls out his silver cigarette case with his initials SS on the right corner, and he removes a Black Djarum cigarette.

He tilts his head slightly to the left. The moonlight shines on his face, and his blue eyes glow brightly as he strokes his lighter with his long, elegant fingers. The lighter lights up and the sensual dark smell of the black clove and cinnamon cigarette smoke swirls around him.

Sorath inhales deeply and narrows his eyes, nodding to himself. *It's almost time for my guests to arrive and I'm going to look for my innocent sacrificial virgin later this evening. I know where she lives.*

He hears steps behind him and slowly smiles up at William, extending his hand to him.

"My Pet, I'm thrilled to see that you arrived early. I love every minute that we spend together but tonight I need to review my plans. I need you to help me capture my sacrificial lamb for the sacrificial ritual this weekend."

William takes his hand and takes the next step down. He stands on the step above the one on which Sorath is standing. He smiles weakly down at Sorath, nodding.

William inhales deeply. Briefly, he closes his beautiful green eyes, and fists his hands against his sides. With determination, he opens his eyes and gazes into Sorath's blue glowing eyes. He smiles weakly down at him, releasing his hand.

"I arrived early because I'm going to ask you to release your bond on me. I'm engaged and I made a commitment prior to our union."

"Never!"

"Sorath, I'll still back you and support your campaign but I can't live like this. I can't be unfaithful to my fiancée!"

He raises his shaking right hand up to his head and slides his fingers through his hair. He moves his shoulders back and raises his chin up in a defiant angle, and glares at him. He moves his shoulders back, and stands straighter, squinting his green eyes. He moves his right hand down and rests it on his waist. He challenges him, and waits for his denial.

"My Pet, I'll never allow you to leave me because we are one. You know that you're my mate! I can't and won't live without!"

Sorath flips his cigarette with his fingers onto the sand. He reaches over to William and grabs his left arm. He pulls William towards him to kiss him deeply and thoroughly. His other hand moves to grasp his neck and holds him close. He ruthlessly kisses him, taking his objections away, and fueling his desire.

William groans and returns the kiss, lost in their passion. *Hell no! I have to step back from this insane consuming passion.*

William moves his hands up to Sorath's shoulders and pushes him back. He glares at him, trembling, with his lips swollen.

"I need you to remove this insane bond, I need to live a normal life with my fiancée. I can't be your mate."

He waits for him to register and grant him his request.

Sorath grins, his blue eyes glow, and he raises his hand to touch his jaw. He slides his thumb over his swollen red lips.

"My Pet, I can't. You're my mate. You will always come to me regardless if you marry. You will always desire my love and our passion. You're bonded to me with the strength of invisible chains."

"No!"

William moves. He turns slightly to take a step up. "I'm not. I'm going to the house to wait for the Senators."

Sorath drops his hand to his side and allows him to leave. He watches William walk up the steps to his home.

Samyaza looks at the entrance of El Matador, waiting for Apollyon. He holds onto Crystal's hand tightly and glances down at her quickly. He smiles a small sexy smile and looks back to the entrance of the cave.

"I'm not sure how and when it opens, but both times it happened around this time."

Crystal whispers, leaning in closer to him. She rests her hand on his chest and encircles his waist with her left arm. Her huge hazel eyes search for the portal.

The sky turns that special faint gray purple color in the horizon, at twilight. The portal opens and Apollyon's hand pushes forward towards Samyaza and Crystal.

His huge frame walks through the portal and Shasi follows him. Her long silky black ponytail swings side to side across her firm ass.

Lyon stops in front of Samyaza, nods, and looks over at Crystal, raising his right eyebrow in question.

"Brother, I'm pleased to see that you're well. I was concerned about your wellbeing. I had to talk Lucifer into backing off."

Crystal's color drains from her face and her beautiful hazel eyes open wide. She blinks quickly, leaning in to Samyaza as she turns to look at Shasi.

"Lyon, I barely made it. My sweet mate was here and she saved me. This is Crystal Bryant. I'll tell you all about it in a while because I think that we should leave."

"Hi." Crystal waves at Lyon and Shasi.

Lyon nods at her and he glances quickly behind him at the portal, and turns to look over at Shasi.

Shasi stands a couple of feet away from him, watching Crystal and Samyaza. The red specks in her eyes sparkle and she smiles.

"Sam, this is Shasi, my faithful warrior. I don't believe that you ever met her."

Samyaza looks over at her and nods, squinting his eyes. "Hi Shasi. He glares at Lyon. "She's a shapeshifter?"

"Yeah."

"Right, why would you allow her to leave the Citadel and enter the earth realm? You know that she can't survive here."

Lyon nods and looks over at Shasi. He shrugs and turns to look at Crystal. *I don't know if I can speak clearly and tell him.*

"Lyon, my mate knows about us."

"Yeah? Right, well earth has several other entities that are not from any of our realms. I know that there're other shapeshifters on the earth realm. I'll tell you about them later. I feel that at this moment we need to go to my apartment in the supernatural building."

"Ok, whatever you feel is right to do. The world has changed since I was here."

Samyaza smiles down at Crystal, holding her closer into his side.

"I bet it was a shock for you, Sam. I felt bad leaving you the way I did but I had to stop Lucifer. I'm pleased that everything turned out. We need to prepare and search for the other Watchers, the angels. I need all of you, I need to release them to fight the Dark Prince."

"Yes, I'm in, Lyon. I want to help you release my brethren."

"Great, I'm going to get my truck. I want you to follow me to the Hell's Night Club. It's located in outskirts of the city adjacent to the mountainside.

The building is an apartment complex for the supernatural entities but also has several floors of different recreational use. The building has several floors that play different music, a theater, as well as several different restaurants.

The supernatural own a few similar structures around the world on the earth realm for their entertainment."

"That sounds very intriguing. I would love to meet these beings. Crystal has a car and she will follow you."

Lyon nods and smiles at them. "Right, we'll be there in a few minutes. It's not far from here."

The twilight has passed and the sky is dark. The moon illuminates the beach.

Lyon turns and walks towards the wooden stairs and Shasi follows behind him.

Crystal raises her eyebrow and looks over at them and then at Sam.

"Yazy, I'm so confused and overwhelmed."

Samyaza smiles down her tenderly and holds her close. He raises his right hand and moves the long silky black strands of hair back from her face. He leans down and kisses her nose.

"Sweetness, don't be afraid because I won't allow anyone to hurt you. I'm gaining my powers by the minute. I'm a very powerful angel."

Crystal eyes widen and she smiles up at him. "Oh, but you don't have wings or do you?"

Samyaza throws back his head and laughs. He looks down at her, shaking his head.

"No, the Watchers don't have wings but the other ranking angels do."

"Oh."

Her lips form a perfect o. Her eyes roam all over his gorgeous face. She nods, smiling up at him.

"Sweetness, we need to hurry."

"Yes."

Samyaza takes her hand and they turn to follow Apollyon and Shasi.

They walk up the wooden stairs and into the parking lot.

Lyon takes long urgent strides towards his truck and opens the door. He pulls it open for Shasi and waits for her to enter.

Shasi stands next to Apollyon, her huge eyes wary, looking at the pickup. She turns to look at Lyon, shaking her head.

"Master, what is this? I don't know what you want me to do?"

Lyon grins at her and extends his right arm to point at the seat.

"Shasi, you need to slide onto the seat and I'll close the door. Don't worry, nothing will happen to you."

He throws back his head, laughing, and turns to look down at her, grinning at her stunned face.

"Shasi, now!"

"Yes, Master!" Shasi squeaks and nervously enters the pickup.

Lyon holds the door, waiting until she slides into the seat, then closes the door.

Samyaza and Crystal walk past them, grinning at Shasi and Lyon.

Lyon and walks around the pickup. He opens his door and slides into his seat, grinning over at Shasi.

"You see. It's not bad at all."

Shasi inhales deeply and clenches her jaw to control her burst of flames. She nods at him and watches him buckle up.

"Shasi, buckle up like this."

She nods and reaches for the seatbelt to buckle up. She crosses her hands on her lap and watches Lyon turn the truck on. The loud sound of his truck startles her.

"Master, this thing roars!"

"Yes."

Lyon glances quickly over at her. He winks at her and shifts the gears to pull out of the parking spot.

"Shasi, relax. It's only going to be a few moments. We'll get to the supernatural building and I'll get the key to my apartment. I'm going to ask that you stay in the building. It's really an amazing building. You won't be bored. I stayed in my apartment a few decades ago and I loved it."

"Yes, Master, I will honor your bidding."

Lyon nods and focuses on driving. He looks in the rearview mirror searching for Samyaza and Crystal. He nods his head when he sees Crystal's Honda behind his truck.

"Damn, Samyaza found his mate instantly. That's totally unreal. I never even thought that we could mate. Is this something new?"

He turns onto the freeway, driving down the coast of Southern California. He turns onto the side of the mountainside and into the huge parking lot of the supernatural building. He pulls into the parking garage and slides next to the little black box.

The green laser beam scans his eyes and the garage doors slide open.

Apollyon drives his trunk inside the parking garage and Crystal follows him inside. She barely makes it inside the garage. The huge silver doors closed tight, locking them inside.

Crystal's huge hazel eyes widen and she drives up next to Lyon's truck in a parking stall. The parking stall garage door appears after she pulls in. She turns to look over at Samyaza, biting her lower lip nervously.

Samyaza looks at her. He leans in close, and kisses her temple.

"Don't worry Sweetness. I won't allow anything or anyone to harm you."

Crystal nods, and smiles up at him weakly. She turns to look as Lyon helps Shasi get out of the truck.

She opens her car door and slides out. She turns to look over at Samyaza as he stands next to the car door.

"Follow me into my apartment. I'm going to order some food because I'm starving."

Samyaza nods and takes Crystal's hand. They follow Lyon into his apartment.

Lyon walks over to the little button on the wall and orders some food. He then turns around to look at Shasi fidget near the huge glass wall.

He walks over to her and stands next to her. He points to the ocean and the mountains.

"Shasi, I'm not going to be here for a while because I'm going to search for the Watchers, the angels. I'm going to ask you to stay near the mountains and inside the building. The building has several restaurants where you can get food and other entertainment."

Shasi turns her head, nodding she looks at Lyon. "Master, what are restaurants and entertainment?"

"Yeah, well, I'm going to you take you on a quick tour."

Shasi nods and looks over at Lyon and Crystal. She smiles at them and turns to look out into the ocean.

"Ok, now I need to figure out where and how I'm going to get the direction of who I'm going to release next. I know that I have to look for my next clue."

Crystal smiles and clasps her hands excitedly. "Omg, I love puzzles. What type of clues are you searching for?"

Lyon glances over at Crystal and nods. "I really don't know. The glyphs appeared in different places but mostly on walls. Yeah! That's it, I must look at the walls."

"Lyon, we can go outside to look?"

Lyon nods at her, and looks out the glass window into the ocean, frowning.

"Yes, but it could be useless. I think it will appear whenever it's the right time to appear." He shrugs his huge shoulders.

The doorbell rings and he turns to look over at the door. He takes long quick strides, his huge leather-shrouded feet sinking deeply into the soft carpet. He crosses the room towards the door.

Lyon opens the door and a young werewolf stands behind a cart full of delicious smelling food. Lyon pulls the door wider and steps back, allowing the waiter to push the cart inside.

"Hi."

"Hi, please place the food on the table."

"Will do." The young waiter sets up the table and turns to leave with the cart.

Lyon raises his eyebrows and nods as he walks out of the apartment. He looks over at Shasi, Sam and Crystal.

"I suggest that we eat to build up our strength. I'm very limited on my powers."

He walks over to the table and pulls off the platter covers. He looks at the food and pulls out his chair, nodding to the others. He starts to serve his plate and looks over at them.

"It's really good. Come on over and eat."

Lyon walks down towards the elevators and turns to look at Samyaza and Crystal. Shasi follows right behind them. She quickly scans her surroundings. They stop next to Lyon and look at the elevator doors.

"I'm going to give you a quick tour, Shasi. I want to introduce you a couple of friends, in case you need anything."

Shasi stands next to Apollyon and nods. She looks at the doors, waiting to see what happens.

The elevator doors open and Lyon walks inside. He motions for them to follow. He quickly explains to Shasi how it works and they stop on several floors. He shows her the restaurants, the theatre, and the different clubs.

He grins at her and nods at his friends that are at the entrance of the Hell's Night club.

"Shasi, please be careful because there are a lot of different entities here. I know that these males will be here in a few to meet you."

Shasi eyes widen and she turns to look inside the dark club. Her eyes adjust to the dark club and she clearly sees all the males turn to look over at her and Crystal.

Samyaza pulls Crystal closer to his side and glares at the other males.

"Master, you need not worry. I can take care of Shasi."

She nods then tilts her head slightly to the side, raising her chin up defiantly, challenging them to come near.

Lyon laughs and looks out into the club. He shrugs his shoulders and turns to walk towards the bar to talk to Baxter McKenzie. He's one of the supernatural attorneys on the earth realm.

The supernatural beings avoid socializing with the humans in order to circumvent any accidental exposure. The club is full of supernatural beings having fun, dancing and drinking.

This club is the favorite haunt of the supernatural entities. Humans are allowed to enter the club, but only with a supernatural escort.

The strong rock music blasts in the room, pumping up the mood and blood in their bodies.

The Hell's Night club is located across from the ocean front in southern California.

Samyaza, Crystal, and Shasi follow him, weaving around the crowd. Crystal's eyes are huge, taking in every single detail.

Samyaza grins. He follows Lyon, pulling Crystal behind him.

Shasi follows them, the red specks in her eyes sparkle taking in the different beings. Her face is flushed and her long ponytail swings across her ass.

Baxter sits at the bar, drinking his favorite golden liquid, whiskey. He watches the cute demonesses that dance with his sister Cynthia.

His dark brown hair shines with highlights in the bar's spotlights and he smiles, tapping his fingers on the counter top. His amazing golden-brown eyes glow, roaming all over the sexy bodies dancing to the wild and loud rock beat.

"Baxter, how are you doing?" Lyon slides onto the bar stool next to him.

Samyaza and Crystal stand a few feet from him. Shasi stops next to Lyon, waiting for his direction.

Baxter turns to look at Lyon, frowning. "Well, it's about fucking time that you turn up. We've been searching for you for quite a while. You know that the supernatural realms council want us to hand you the key to hell."

"I told you that it isn't my domain and Lucifer is the man you want. I don't understand how this council wants to force this on me. I'm not part of their realms and they have no jurisdiction over me. They don't have a clue of who I am."

Baxter takes his glass from the bar counter top and takes a drink of his whiskey. He shrugs his wide shoulders and turns to glare at Lyon.

"I don't know and I don't care. We need to give you the key so I can get them off our backs."

Baxter glances over at Samyaza, Crystal, and Shasi. He raises his eyebrows and looks at Lyon.

"You have a human in here and two beings that I can't recognize."

Lyon smiles. He leans against the counter, and then leans in closer.

"Baxter I need your help. I need you to keep an eye on Shasi."

Baxter frowns. He looks over at Crystal and Shasi. He shakes his head and looks at Lyon.

"I can't. I don't babysit." He looks down at his glass and swirls the whisky around his glass, brooding.

"Really, Baxter, I need you to keep an eye on her. She doesn't have a clue about this realm or about anything here. I really have to go on an urgent errand. It's extremely crucial for the existence of humanity."

Baxter looks up at Lyon, raising his right eyebrow. "That sounds fucking unreal. I'll keep an eye on her if you stop by the office in a few hours to take the key. That's the only condition."

Lyon scowls and turns to look over at Samyaza and then Shasi. He grinds his molars and nods.

"Very well, I'll take this damn key but I'm telling you that the council is wrong."

Baxter shrugs and takes a drink. He leans back against the bar top and smiles at Lyon.

"I don't care. We just want them off our backs. You deal with it."

"Damn you, Baxter. But you're going to deal with keeping my warrior out of trouble."

Baxter crosses his arms and shakes his head. *Fucking hell, how did I get screwed like this? I don't have time to take care of this girl!*

"I need you to know that she's a shapeshifter and very powerful. Don't antagonize her because I'm not responsible for her actions."

Baxter glances over at Shasi with new interest. His eyes roam all over her beautiful face and stops to stare at her full red lips. His eyes slowly roam down to look at her full breasts, down her small waist, and her long sexy legs. His blood rushes through is body in a fiery burn.

"Stay away from her Baxter because she can be extremely mean."

"Oh yeah?"

Baxter gaze moves up to look into her beautiful eyes. He gazes into her eyes, falling deep into her soul. *Hell she's a beauty. Damn, I can feel her soul reaching out for mine. Oh hell no! I'm not falling, I can't. I don't have time for this. It wouldn't work, she's not a werewolf so it can't happen.* He blinks and turns away.

He scowls, grinds his molars, and glances over at Lyon.

"Don't worry, I'll take care of her." He grumbles, nodding at him.

"Great, because she's staying in my apartment and I need you to help her if she needs it."

"Right, no worries. Here's my business card. Give it to her so she can call me. I'll be expecting you early in the morning."

Baxter stands from the bar and takes out a few bills to place on the counter. He looks over at Samyaza and Crystal. He nods at them and turns to smile at Shasi.

"See ya."

He turns around and walks out of the club, forgetting all about Lyon and ignoring Shasi's eyes in his mind. He looks down at his cell phone, frowning.

Lyon looks at Samyaza and nods. He gets up from the bar stool and walks out of the club with them following him.

Sorath drives his black Audi down the coast with William next to him. William is clenching his fists, frustrated at his control and his lack of will to resist. He looks out of the window, looks at the wave crash along the beach. His eyes roam all over the landscape, searching for answers.

"My Pet, I don't understand why you're fighting our union. I won't allow you to leave me."

William turns to look at him. His eyes narrow in a furious squint. He shakes his head and turns to look out of the car glass.

"How in the world do you think it's going to be so easy to take this woman? What do you mean about sacrificial lamb?"

Sorath grins. He grips the steering wheel tight and glances quickly over at him.

"Yes, she's a woman that I have been keeping an eye on for a while. She's pure and innocent. She's perfect for the sacrificial rite where I'll gain additional power."

William hisses and turns to look away from him. *I can't fucking believe it! He is totally evil, a black heart! Oh yeah the Dark Prince. Damn! I'm under his dominion, no matter how much I fight it. He's totally in control and owns my soul. It damn fucking unreal. I know what and who he is and I can't resist him. I know that nobody can save me now. I don't have a soul.*

William closes his eyes tight and attempts to erase Carol's questioning eyes from his mind and conscience.

Sorath turns off the freeway and onto the street. He drives down the different streets until he reaches Crystal's apartment. He drives into the parking lot searching for her car. He frowns and looks down at his watch.

"Damn it! She's not here and it's the middle of the night."

Sorath searches the parking lot, tapping his right hand fingers on the steering wheel. He turns to the far left to look into the dark corner. He frowns and shrugs.

"She's not home because her car is not here. I'm going to have to return later and take her in the morning. I need to get her before tomorrow night."

William crosses his arms and looks out into the parking lot.

Later that evening, close to the break of dawn, Lyon and Samyaza walk into the McKenzie, McKenzie, and Jones Law firm in Southern California. They open the wooden door and walking into the reception area.

Baxter is sitting in his black leather chair, leaning back and looking out the glass wall that separates his office and the reception area. His back is to the huge window that frames the beach. He watches Lyon and Samyaza enter the reception area and taps his fingers on the black desk.

Lyon looks at Baxter through the glass wall. He nods at him and continues towards the glass door.

Baxter raises his hand to wave at them to enter his office.

Lyon opens the glass door and walks into Baxter's office. Samyaza follow him in, closing the door.

"Hey, I'm here."

"Fucking happy to see that you came to get this damn key!"

Lyon looks around and walks over to take a seat in front of the desk. He leans back and crosses his arms.

Samyaza nods at Baxter and takes the other seat, resting his hands on the armchair.

Baxter grins. He leans forward to grab the silver box that contains the silver hell key. He hands it to Lyon.

"Here!" He smiles leaning back into his chair, crossing his arms.

"Damn it!"

Lyon scowls, and leans forward to take the silver box. He looks down at it, shaking his head at the silver box and reads the glyphs on the lid.

"The Key To The Watchers Hell Chamber"

He opens the box and looks down at the silver key nestled in the red velvet cushion. He takes the huge silver key out of the box. He moves his hand up and down, weighing the key, raising his eyebrows.

"The key is heavy."

He raises the silver key closer to read the intricate glyphs written on it. He frowns and shakes his head.

How in the hell did this happen? I thought that Lucifer ruled Hell. This key has to be the key to a parallel zone in Hell. Fuck, this isn't part of the stations. How fucking incredible is that? No wonder I never detected the Watchers, the angels aura!

He turns the huge eight inch silver key over to read the intricate glyphs embossed on the key shank. The bow of the key has beautiful crown with wings. The crown has dark red rubies.

Lyon reads the glyphs on the shank. Samyaza leans over and forward to look over his shoulders.

"This key opens the eternal penance chambers that incarcerates the Watchers, the fallen angels. Holy God, holy and strong, holy and immortal, have mercy upon us."

"I don't see anything but some intricate scroll work." Samyaza frowns and leans back into the chair, glancing over at Baxter.

Lyon looks up from the key to look at him, frowning.

"Really? You can't read it?"

"Yeah."

Lyon turns to look at Baxter, standing up. He smiles at him, nodding.

"Thanks for the key, Baxter. I'll call to get an update on Shasi."

"Yeah, no worries." Baxter stands squinting, resting his hands on his waist. He looks confused and curious about the strange inscription on the key.

"Later, dude." Samyaza grins and stands from the chair.

"Yeah." Baxter nods, raising his hand to rub his jaw.

Lyon and Samyaza walk out of his office and into the reception area. They exit the law office and walk towards Lyon's truck. They enter the truck and Lyon starts it and pulls away from the curb.

He grabs onto the steering wheel tightly and glances over at Sam.

"I believe that the signs are meant for me. I hope that you're not planning on taking your mate with us to search for the angels. That would be insane."

Samyaza closes his beautiful violet eyes and then looks at him, raising his right eyebrow.

"Yeah, I do want to but I know it's going to be dangerous. I'm going to ask her to wait for me at her apartment."

He pulls into the parking garage and drives into his parking stall. They exit the truck and walk into Lyon's apartment.

Lyon nods and smiles. He looks over at Shasi and Crystal, sitting outside on the balcony. He takes the silver key from the silver box and slides it inside his leather jacket.

He places the box on the book shelf. He smiles and walks towards the balcony.

"Let's go and give them the instructions. I need to start looking for more signs to locate the next angel."

Samyaza stops and pulls him back. He glares at him, shaking his head.

"I need to talk to Crystal, so I'm leaving now to her apartment. Give me a few to talk to her."

Lyon raises his right eyebrow and nods. He pulls his arm, grinning.

"Yeah, I'll be there in a few."

"Thanks."

Nine

Sorath walks down the walkway towards Crystal's apartment complex. He walks past the gate and up the staircase to the last apartment. He knocks on the door and turns to look around the top floor. He shrugs and smiles, pulling out his business card.

He turns around as Crystal opens the door and smiles. He extends his right hand in greeting and hands her his business card with his left hand. He smiles at her, charming and nice. He uses his power to entice her and make her feel safe.

"Hi Ms. Bryant, I'm Senator Sorath Santanel. I'm running for President of the United States. I decided to reach out to my constituents and I'm here to personally invite you to my campaign dinner party. I understand that you're a paramedic for the Los Angeles Paramedic department. I would be honored to have you attend as a representative for your department."

Crystal's eyes widen. She bites her lower lip, confused and excited. She blushes deeply and nods.

"Oh my, that really is amazing Senator Santanel! I've been following the candidates and omg, I can't believe it!"

Sorath nods and steps back, grinning, enjoying her excitement. He crosses his arms, nodding at her comments.

"I'm pleased to learn that you're interested in the candidates."

Crystal face flushes and she nods. "Yes, I am interested in this election."

"Nice to meet you, Crystal. I'll be waiting for you this evening."

Sorath hands her an elegant invitation. It has a black background with an intricate insignia and silver letters. The invitation is simple, yet elegant.

Crystal nods and looks down. Her eyes quickly read the elegant invitation card. She looks back at him, sliding the card into her jean pocket.

"I'll be there, Senator Santanel. Thank you for your invitation."

He nods and turns to walk away, grinning with satisfaction.

Oh yeah, there's nothing better than to have them come willingly into my dominion. I don't have to force her to attend the dinner party.

Crystal closes the door, smiling, and shakes her head. I can't believe that I acted like a teenage girl. Geeze, it's just so exciting to meet the Senator of my district. I can't believe that I was selected and I'm off today!! Oh yeah!!

Samyaza is out for a while and geeze, I don't have a reason not to attend this epic moment.

She runs to her room and pulls open her closet door. She shoves her dresses back and forth on the clothes rod.

"Oh wow, I don't know if I have anything decent to wear."

She walks over to her dresser and pulls out the invitation. She places it on her dresser along with her car keys.

She turns around and walks back to her closet to start trying on her limited dresses.

Lyon and Samyaza search for signs everywhere but don't see any. Lyon clenches his molars, frustrated. He clenches his fists, and glares. He turns to look darkly at Samyaza, shaking his head.

"I can't believe that I can't see anything. I don't know where to look. The few times that I have seen these scriptures have been unexpected and unusual sites."

Samyaza leans against the street light in the downtown area. He crosses his arms, shaking his head.

"Maybe you're trying too hard. Maybe you need to relax and then they will be evident to you."

Lyon closes his beautiful swirling eyes and pulls on his sunglasses since it's now the early morning. The sunshine is bright and he doesn't want to have the humans notice his eyes. He frowns. He looks at Samyaza's violet eyes and turns around. He walks into the small liquor store, then over to the rack of sunglasses and he takes a pair off the rack. He goes over to the counter.

The young male stands behind the counter, playing on his cell phone. He never looks up from the cell. He takes the sunglasses from Lyon. He scans the tag on the sunglasses, and shoves them into the paper bag. He takes Lyon's debit card, and slides the card, and hands it back to Lyon without looking at them. He only focuses on the cell phone and register.

Lyon shakes his head and grunts. He takes the bag and card back.

"Thanks."

He turns around and walks out of the liquor store, grinning.

Samyaza follows him, looking around the small liquor store with curiosity. He then turns around to follow Lyon out of the store.

"What is that place, what did he do, and why did you go inside? You really need to explain stuff to me because everything is totally different and unusual."

Lyon laughs and pulls the sunglasses from the paper bag. He rips off the tags and hands the glasses to Samyaza.

"Here, put these on. It's not as if the humans have eyes our color. We don't want to cause any fear, or draw attention."

"Right. I didn't think about that. I remember when we first descended from the heavens and our eyes caused fear and confusion."

"I want to walk around for a while and then we'll take a small break. I can't give up the search because we need to gather our powers. Who knows what that fiend Sorath Santanel, the Dark Prince, is up to but I know it's not good. He's only gaining power and wants to have control over the United States."

"Right."

Samyaza and Lyon walk down the streets, looking for any leads and trying to appear normal. They walk up and down the downtown streets and parks.

After a few hours, Lyon stops and looks at his cell phone. "Damn it, it's late and I'm starving. Let's get something to eat and then we can continue our search."

"Ok." Samyaza nods and he looks around the street trying to figure out how and where they are going to get some food.

"I know of this small amazing restaurant that you're going to love. Sam, the food is a lot better now than back then. The humans have evolved without the Watchers angels' help!"

He laughs at Samyaza, slaps him on the back, and starts to walk down towards the restaurant.

A little while later, Lyon hands Samyaza a new cell phone. Samyaza looks at the new slim, shiny, rectangular, glass-looking object. He looks over at Lyon, raising his right eyebrow. He waves the cell, lifts his chin, and with a quizzical look, asks "Yeah? What is it?"

Lyon takes back the cell phone, laughing. "Wow, yeah, you don't have a clue. Geeze, I've been on the earth realm from the inception of every evolution in every area. This is called a cell phone and I'll explain it in more detail later. What you need to know right now is that you can call me with it or anyone else."

Samyaza laughs, throwing back his head and then looks back at him.

"Really? I can call you without it!"

Lyon closes his eyes, and shakes his head. "Yeah, but this is used by everyone. Crystal would be able to call you. Stop being such a smart ass and give it a try."

Lyon frowns, running his right hand through his long hair. "Hell Sam, you need to act human, remember."

Samyaza stops laughing, nods, and takes back the cell phone. He slides it inside the pocket on the side of the new black leather jacket that Crystal bought him.

"We're going to look around for a while longer and then we should return to the apartment to look closer at the key. Maybe I missed a clue."

"Right."

Crystal brushes out her long hair and sets the hairbrush on the dresser. She leans forward to pull the silver hoops from the small jewelry box.

She smiles and tilts her head to the side. Her long glossy hair falls in a silky cascade, and she slides the small silver hoop through her pierced earlobe. She turns to the other side and slides that small hoop into place. She smiles and stands straight, looking into the mirror.

"Yes, this little black dress is going to work. Thank god for little black dresses."

She turns away from the mirror and grabs her car keys, leaving behind the invitation. She walks through her room and down the hallway, smiling. She looks at her cell phone to check the time.

She walks down the hallway, and the front door bell buzzes.

"Who could that be?"

She frowns, and walks to the doorway to look through the peephole.

A tall thin man in a black suit stands at the door holding a black hat. He's wearing white gloves and looks like a chauffeur from an old movie.

Crystal laughs, shaking her head and her hair floats around her back in a black cloud.

"This is so fun!"

She opens the door, grinning excitedly. Her face is flushed, and she holds the door open.

"Yes?"

He bows his head and then stands straight, holding his hat in his hands.

"Ms. Bryant, I'm Lurch the chauffeur, and Senator Santanel sent me to collect you. I'm to drive you to the dinner party."

"Ohhh, that so special!"

"Are you ready, Ms. Bryant?"

He asks her in a monotone voice and serious face. He looks at her. His dark brown eyes look deadpan, and his face taut.

Crystal nods She walks over to the armchair beside the door to grab her coat, and she returns to the front door, smiling. She reaches behind the door to turn the lock. She nods, and turns to walk out.

She walks down the narrow walkway, holding her keys and cell phone in one hand. She adjusts her coat on her arm and slides them into her coat side pocket.

The dark navy sky is clear and the moon is full, cushioned among the glowing stars. She nods, and excitedly clutches her coat, beaming as she enters the white Mercedes.

The chauffeur, Lurch, drives down the highway at a moderate speed, passing the slower cars. Crystal looks out the window at the ocean, smiling. She looks down to adjust her dress and then looks up to stare at the huge Tudor house.

The driver drives up the circular driveway and stops in front of the huge wooden doors. He opens the door and slides out of the car. His shiny black shoes tap on the cobblestone driveway as he walks around the car. He reaches for the door handle and opens the door for Crystal.

"Ms. Bryant." He extends his hand to assist her out of the car.

Oh my, this house is huge. I'm so excited and nervous. I know that there will be a lot of politicians. I'm so excited.

She looks up at him and takes his hand and scoots across the seat to slide her right leg out. She gracefully exits the car and smiles at Lurch.

"Thank you, Lurch."

"Welcome, this way."

He closes the door and walks up ahead of her to the front doors. He opens the doors and waves his hand for her to enter the lobby.

"This way, Ms. Bryant."

Crystal nods, her eyes roaming all over the foyer, taking in the paintings and the furniture. She turns around, and extends her neck to look into the huge grand room, already full of elegant guests.

Oh my, I must be crazy. What am I doing here? Oh wow, look at the huge crystal chandelier! It's so beautiful. I absolutely love crystal and I love how this one has so many facets. .

The chauffeur, Lurch, continues to walk down the hall and down the stairs. He stops at the last step, waiting for her.

Crystal walks down the stairs, holding on to the polished wooden rail, looking all over the grand room. Her eyes shine brightly and her silky hair glimmers with the light. Her red lips turn up at the corners, as she smiles.

Lurch takes a champagne glass from the waiter's tray. He turns slightly into the curve of the stairway, and slyly spikes the drink with fine white powder. He swirls the champagne and hands it to Crystal.

"Ms. Bryant, enjoy your evening." He stands close to her and waits for her to drink the champagne.

"Thank you."

Crystal takes the glass and starts to walk around to the back of the grand room, taking a few sips.

She stands halfway from the back french doors that lead to the garden and the front door. She leans against the one of the doors on the side of wall.

Omg, there he is. Oh yeah, look at the other handsome senator, and he's one of my favorite Senator's. Senator William Jackson. I should have applied for an internship at the capitol. I love the world of politics and I only get a glimpse every once in a while at work.

Crystal takes another sip of her champagne and leans against the door frame, feeling relaxed. She watches Senator Sorath walk towards her, grinning. She smiles and nods at Senator Sorath Santanel's greeting.

Sorath stops in front of her, smiling, and raising his right hand forefinger, signaling it will be a second. He turns to place his whisky glass on the tray that the waiter is holding.

"Ms. Bryant, it's a pleasure to see that you decided to accept my invitation. I see that you're enjoying yourself."

Crystal nods and takes a sip of champagne. "I'm thrilled to be here. I find the campaign and politics fascinating. I would love to meet the Senators."

Sorath laughs. His perfect white teeth gleam, and his blue eyes glow as he nods. He takes her arm.

"Allow me to introduce you."

They take a few steps and then Crystal starts to feel dizzy. He wraps his arm around her waist and pulls her up.

"Oh!"

The older couple standing next to them turn their heads and stare at them. Their eyes widen and their mouth drop open. Mr. Lender and Mrs. Lender gasp as they watch Crystal start to fall.

Sorath nods at them, and smiles. "No worries, I'm sure she's going to be ok."

The Dark Prince pulls her close and walks over a few steps to go into his office. He opens the door and walks into his office with her. He closes and locks the door and places her on the arm chair.

"Oh yes, I finally have my sacrificial lamb in my domain. I'm going to take her to my altar. I can't wait to start my ritual."

He leans down and pushes back her hair from her face to grasp her chin. He moves her face to the left and right, nodding.

"Yes, she's going to have to do because I know that she's not a virgin anymore! Damn it!"

He backs away from her, frowning, and stands staring at her with his hands on his waist.

"What the hell!! Fuck it! I'm going to have to use her even if she's not pure. I'll still gain power, not as much as the plan but something is good."

He shrugs his shoulders and turns to walk over to the bookcase and slides his hand over the decorative scroll on the bookcase. The bookcase slides to the left and stops when it reaches the wall.

A small hallway is exposed. There is a black wooden door without a handle. The door is closed. Sorath waves his hand and the door slides open. The stairway walls are made of rock and several fire lamps are attached to the ceiling, hanging from black chain. The fire dances, casting eerie shadows and sending a thick layer of smoke down the stairway.

The Dark Prince smiles and turns around to walk back to scoop her into his arms. He then turns to walk down the stairway.

He goes down the stairs and stops at the last step. The strong spicy incense cones burn at the altar. The room is satiated with pungent sexy spicy cinnamon incense. The cinnamon is used to inflame the senses, causing passion and lust to run unbridled in a heady powerful need of desire. It's a strong aphrodisiac, quite useful in the powerful fire energy ritual.

He looks over at the altar nodding. He takes the last step down and walks across the room towards the altar. He stops at the side of the altar, leans down, and places Crystal on the table.

Sorath looks at her, smiling, as he slides off her high heel shoes. He then grabs the hem of her dress and pushes it up and over her head.

He looks down at her huge breasts. He then tears off her small black bikini, grinning. He pulls her hands up and ties them with the red silk rope.

He runs his hands down her body caressing her huge breasts and massaging down her legs. He takes her ankle and ties it up with the red silk rope. He then ties the other ankle, watching her breathe. He turns around, grinning in satisfaction, and walks up the stairs.

Samyaza and Lyon walk up the stairway towards Crystal's apartment. They walk to the door and Samyaza grabs the door knob and tries to turn the door knob. He frowns and looks over at Lyon.

"She's not home, I can't feel her."

Lyon stands next to him, crossing his arms, and raising his right eyebrow.

Samyaza waves his hand over the door knob to unlock the door. He grabs the door knob and opens the door. He walks into the small living room, looking for her.

Lyon follows him inside and turns to close the front door. He stands in the living room, looking around. *I don't feel any other auras here.*

"Sweetness, I'm home."

He walks down the hallway towards Crystal's room. He walks inside the bedroom and waves his hand to turn the lights on. He looks around the room and walks over to the bathroom. He looks inside, then turns around clenching his hands.

"Hell, I feel this pressure in my chest. She's feels anxious and scared. Where did she go?" He walks over to her dresser to look around. He sees the invitation and reads it. He raises his right eyebrow shaking his head.

"This invitation is from Sorath Santanel, the Dark Prince. What the fuck is going on?"

He turns around and storms out of her bedroom and down the hall, furiously stomping into the dark brown carpet. The floor shakes and creaks.

Lyon turns to look at him, squinting his eyes.

"What's up?"

Samyaza stops in front of him and extends his long muscular arm to hand him the invitation.

"I don't understand what's going on, Lyon. Look at this invitation. It looks like Crystal went. I see evidence of her dressing for this dinner party."

Lyon takes the invitation and reads it. "What the hell! This is a dinner party from the Dark Prince. How in the hell did he locate her and why? Does he know that are on him? This is fucking incredible!"

Samyaza's beautiful violet eyes glow and he grinds his molars, flexing the muscle on his face.

"I have to get her out of his clutches, Apollyon! I can feel her fear. Who knows what he's doing to my mate."

Lyon looks up, his swirling gray-blue eyes shimmer and he nods.

"Let's get her! I'll drive down to his home. We can do this together. I'm not sure if we can overpower him but we can stop him."

"Right." Samyaza nods, following Lyon out of the apartment.

Lyon walks towards his car, unable to flash, and Samyaza follows him. They pull the truck doors in unison and slide onto the seats. Lyon quickly exits the parking lot, pushing down on the gas pedal. He drives crazy and fast, using powers to turn the lights green and stop other cars as he races down the streets, anxious to get to the freeway.

A few moments later, he drives his truck down the road on the coastline towards Sorath's house. They look around the property and at the parked cars all around the circular driveway and down the both sides of the street. The Tudor lights shine brightly from inside. You can see people standing around in groups, talking and laughing, through the huge glass windows.

Samyaza closes his eyes. He inhales deeply, and searches for her aura. He shakes his head and fists his shaking hands.

"She's in there but not with the party. I feel her somewhere in the house but I can't see her aura."

Lyon nods and looks at the house, extending his limited sensors. He closes his eyes to focus and then opens them, frustrated. He sighs and shakes his head.

"Samyaza, I can't help you because I'm very limited in my powers. I did receive a small dose when I released you but I still can't do much. Hell!"

"Right." Samyaza looks over at the huge Tudor house. He squints, his upper lid twitches, and his eyes zooms in closer to search for Crystal.

Lyon nods towards the guards at the front of the house. He leans in closer to whisper to Samyaza.

"We can't get from the front with those guards standing there. I'll walk up from the back of the house and walk inside. I'll search the first floor."

"Right. I can flash to that balcony over there and I'll search the top floor. Maybe once I'm in the house I can locate her aura."

"We need to get her out without confronting the Dark Prince. I don't want to alert him of our existence. I know that he couldn't detect me when I was next to him. I hope that he can't detect you."

"Right. I hope not. It would be to our advantage to have him unaware of us. I know that he can't sense you but I'm not sure about me, Apollyon. It would be great if he doesn't sense our aura."

Lyon nods and starts to walk towards the back and jumps onto the beach. He walks down, searching for a way up. He looks at the side of the cliff, frowning, and continues walking towards the back. He looks around for a way up.

There has to be a way up. Any owner would have a way down to the beach. It's only logical. It's not like he doesn't have the money to make one.

He looks to the side of the rocky cliff and nods. *Yeah, there it is. He walks towards the stairs on the side of the cliff to Sorath's property. He takes quick steps up the stairs.*

Samyaza flashes to the balcony on the second floor of the huge Tudor home. He leans against the wall and creeps up to the huge french doors. He looks inside and grins.

Yeah, it's empty. I'm flashing inside. Maybe I can feel my sweet Crystal. He flashes into the room and looks around. The room is empty but he's in Sorath's bedroom.

Samyaza raises his right eyebrow, looking at the huge dark maple bed. The bedspread is a dark blood red satin with black floral petals and leaves embroidered around the edge.

The Prince and his black aura assault his equilibrium. He closes his eyes to try to fight off the offensive aura and keep his focus on Crystal and his feelings for her.

The Dark Prince aura is devastatingly strong and I know that only one angel alone wouldn't be enough to stop him. I understand what Apollyon means. Our combine powers are the one and only way to destroy this beast.

He allows his mind to reach out. His soul seeks Crystal's soul, and scouts for her heartbeat. His blood runs rapidly through his body as he fights off the overpowering dark aura, and his face has a fine sheen of sweat. He clenches his jaw tight, the muscle flex on the side of his pale face, and he opens his beautiful violet eyes.

I feel her but I can't locate the exact spot so I can flash. I have to get to her.

Samyaza flashes into the hallway and he walks down the hall, stopping at each room to search for her.

He clenches his hands tight and continues down the stairway, hugging the wall, and searching for a place to flash. He stops when he sees two men talking at the bottom of the stairway.

He squints his eyes, his vision zooms in to watch the two men at the base of the stairway talking. *Hell, that's the Dark Prince, Sorath. I can feel his dark aura. What the fuck!*

Samyaza's body tenses, he clenches his jaw tight, and his heart stops as he listens.

"Pet, I have my sacrificial lamb in my chamber. I want you to stay tonight because I want you to witness my ritual after this dinner party is over."

Sorath moves his right hand and grabs William's arm, gazing deeply into his green eyes.

William shakes his head, a dirty blonde lock falls over his forehead, and he turns his face to break their eye contact. He takes a deep drink of his whiskey, swishes the golden liquid around his mouth, and swallows enjoying the burn.

"I told you that I can't. I brought my Fiancée with me!"

Sorath's blue eye glow and he takes a step closer to William. He gazes deep into William's eyes and takes control of him.

Pet, I need you with me and I don't give a damn about your fiancée! You will stay with me because you're mine. I need you by my side! Take her home and then I want you to return immediately to me.

William swallows the huge lump in his throat, understanding and realizing the power that the Dark Prince has over his will. *Fuck, he owns my soul, and controls me. I can't go against his will no matter how much I feel it's wrong. I have to accept that I'm going to hell.*

"Damn you!"

William pulls his arm from Sorath's firm grip and walks off to search for his fiancée Carol.

Sorath stands rooted to the floor, watching William walk away. He takes a drink of his whiskey and nods, smiling at his triumph.

Samyaza frowns, watching Sorath closely. *I see that he controls his disciples and I'm sure that most of the people in this party are under his control. I wonder how I'm going to get into his chamber. I know that's where my Crystal is. It's only logical. I wonder if it is some type of dungeon. Damn it!*

Samyaza leans into the wall, trying to remain unnoticed. He watches Sorath walk away, his eyes roam the room for Apollyon, and he looks back as the Dark Prince walks towards the other side of the room following William.

He walks down the stairway, trying to remain undetected, and not to draw attention to himself.

He reaches the last step and the waiter walks pass him. He extends his arm towards Samyaza.

Samyaza takes a glass of champagne which the waiter offered him, nods his thanks to him, and continues to walk towards the first doors.

I need to get into that first door to see where it goes and to escape this party. I don't want to have them notice me because I'm not dressed for the occasion.

Right, this leather jacket and jeans are not the same. I stick out like a black stain on white cloth.

I need to hurry because I can feel Crystal but I don't feel her emotions.

Samyaza grabs the door knob and turns the knob. He pushes the door open and walks into Sorath's office. He closes the door and leans against it, taking in the furniture.

He looks all over the huge office and then walks over to the bookcase.

I'm positive that this has the door because I'm sure that the secret door must be used in today's world. It's simply logical to use one, especially for what the Dark Prince is doing. He has his disciples in his tight control. I know that he's taken their souls.

Samyaza moves his hands all over the book case starting from the far right working his hands over every shelf, every scroll, and moving the books.

He looks over at the door and then continues his search. He clenches his jaw, his eyes narrow, and he inhales deeply. He slowly exhales to control his anxiety and desperation.

Damn, I smell the strong spicy incense seeping from this area. It's totally old incense that was used in my time. I think that I can flash once I break the seal.

Samyaza shudders, nods, and moves faster to search for the lever to open the bookcase. His left hand softly pushes the scroll and he hears the faint pop.

He closes his eyes and softly exhales, not realizing that he has been holding his breath.

"Right."

He takes a step back to look at the bookcase, which is slightly ajar. He walks quickly over to the door and pulls it open.

"Right, another door. Damn it! Fucking hell. I don't see the door handle."

He moves his hand up to slide it through his black hair. The door opens when he moves his hand in the air.

Samyaza's eyes widen and he grins. *Right, I'm in!* He pulls the huge door open and watches the fire lamps magically light up.

"Right, I'm not walking down the stairs. I can flash now!"

He flashes instantly down to the ritual room. He looks at the altar. He glares, and then scowls. *She's totally naked! Fucking bastard!*

"Fuck!"

He runs over to Crystal and checks her pulse.

"Sweetness, wake up."

He softly and urgently shakes her. He pulls at the silk ties and unties her. He pulls her up into his arms, into a sitting position on the altar.

"Sweetness, please wake. I'm running scared!"

He sees her shallow breathing and frowns. He runs his hands over her pale face and pushes her hair back.

The Dark Prince stops at the last step, he turns to look at Crystal.

"What the fuck! What the hell!"

Samyaza turns to glare at him and lays Crystal softly back on the altar.

"Who are you and how did you get in?"

Sorath walks over to Samyaza taking in every detail. He raises his eyebrow and growls.

"Get your hands off her!"

Samyaza eyes glow and he snarls at him. "The fuck I will. I'm taking her out of here!"

Samyaza's hair raises at the back of his neck, and he flexes his huge biceps as he clenches his hands into tight fists.

Sorath throws back his head laughing, and then he abruptly stops.

"I can't believe that you're challenging me. You don't have a clue of who I am and what I can do to you! I'm going to do you a favor, that's right. I'm going to kill you quickly."

Sorath moves his hand back to magically produce a sword to kill him.

Samyaza squints his eyes and shakes his head. "I tell you what. I'm going to leave with my mate and you're not going to do a thing to stop me."

"You're a crazy ass!"

Sorath swings back the sword and Samyaza flashes. He stands at the other side of the altar and quickly looks down at Crystal.

Crystal is beginning to open her yes and moans. She slowly pushes up into a sitting position on the altar. She moves her hand up to rub her aching head.

"Oh dear, where am I?"

Crystal, shaking, looks at the altar and down at her naked body. She yells, wide eyed and full of terror.

"Sweetness, don't move."

Samyaza grabs the altar-height candlestick, taking off the red candle and tossing it to the side, splattering the hot wax on the floor. He flashes over to Sorath to fight him.

Lurch walks down the stairway with a tray of glasses and wine. He walks into the ritual room and stops.

Sorath glances quickly over at him, his blue eyes glow and he growls.

"Lurch, get the girl!"

Samyaza moves the hand holding the candlestick and swings hard to knock the sword out of Sorath's hand.

Sorath blocks it and laughs at him, shaking his head.

Lurch walks over to the altar and places the tray onto the altar at the end. He reaches for Crystal and takes her into his arms. He holds her, waiting for Sorath to tell him where to take her.

Crystal pushes against his chest, yelling at the top of her lungs, tears falling down her face.

"Let me go!"

"I'm killing you! I'm going for your neck! I don't think I'll go wrong taking your head off!"

Sorath takes a quick step to the side and lurches forward to cut off Samyaza's head.

What the fuck! Where did this maggot come from?

Samyaza watches Lurch take Crystal in his arms and angrily moves to block Sorath.

Damn, the Dark Prince doesn't have a clue who I am but he's knows that I can flash.

Sorath laughs, shaking his head. He shifts his weight and starts to bounce on the sole of his feet, leaning forward ready to pounce.

Samyaza watches William standing at the last step, frowning at the scene. He takes a step down and stands to watch, sliding his hands into his pants pockets.

Samyaza nods and flashes over to William and grabs him from the back, encircling his neck with his right arm.

"I suggest that you tell your huge maggot to take Crystal out of here and up to the front yard."

William face turns red and his eyes water as he stares at Sorath.

Sorath growls. He takes a step closer to Samyaza searching for a way to get to him without hurting William.

"Don't push me into killing your precious man." Samyaza nods at him. "Now!"

Sorath blinks and glances over at Crystal and then at William.

What the fuck! She's not worth me sacrificing my beloved Pet. I can get another sacrificial lamb and I don't know who this dude is. He can flash but I don't sense any special powers. What the fuck! Who in the hell is he? He has to be a demon or something to be able to get inside my ritual chamber. I'll look into it later because right now I'm going to do what he wants.

"Ok, but don't hurt him, you bastard!"

Samyaza tightens his hold on Williams's neck, glaring at Sorath.

"Now!"

"Lurch, do as he said!" Sorath waves his hand and the sword disappears. "Let him go!"

Samyaza grins, shakes his head, and walks back to stand close to the stairs.

"Hurry up and take my mate out of this hell hole!"

He grins at his cute analogy, not! *Yeah, this is not close to what hell is!*

Sorath growls and his blue eyes glow as he looks at William close his eyes.

"Lurch, move! Get the girl out of here!"

"Yes, Master." Lurch takes two steps at a time up the stairs.

"Let him go!" Sorath watches William closely, watching his shallow breathing.

Samyaza nods and releases William. William falls onto the ground, unconscious. Sorath runs over to him, forgetting about Samyaza.

Samyaza instantly flashes up into the office in front of Lurch.

Samyaza takes Crystal out of his arms and flashes out of the room. Crystal wraps her arms around his neck, sobbing uncontrollably.

He lands in the front yard, looking around. He frowns and calls Apollyon. He leans down to kiss her temple softly.

"Shushhhh…….you're safe."

Apollyon! I have her. I'm flashing home!

Lyon stops searching in the huge library. He looks down at the glowing scroll that he's holding in his hand. He frowns and starts to unroll it. He absent-mindedly responds to Sam.

I'll be there in a few, Samyaza.

Apollyon looks at the old scroll's glyphs, shaking his head.

"I can't fucking believe it. I found my next clue."

The hot sand, rocks, and darkness are Azazel's eternal penance. The virtue of humility is your strength and shall be his. The chains are broken, the time is now, and his test to atone to regain heavenly grace. Follow the road, follow the sun, and you shall find Azazel at Redwall Cavern right at twilight.

Fucking yes! Samyaza and I will release Azazel very soon!

He nods and walks over to the French doors. He walks out into the patio, looking for his way to the front.

Lyon turns to walk towards the front yard and glances over at the side of the rocky mountainside.

Apollyon drives into the parking lot and turns off the truck. He walks quickly across the parking lot towards the stair. He holds on tight to the old scroll with his right hand and grabs the stair rail with his left hand. He quickly takes two steps at a time to reach the second floor in a few moments.

He walks to Crystal's apartment and knocks. He looks around the modest apartment complex.

Samyaza opens the door, he waves Lyon inside, and closes the door.

Lyon walks inside and stands next to the slate blue sofa.

"How is she doing?"

"She's sleeping but I had to use some of my powers to calm her down. I can't fucking believe it! That bastard was going to use my mate as a sacrificial lamb!"

"I'm glad that we arrived on time. I'm going to show you the clue that I found in his library. This scroll was laying on the table, glowing. I picked it up and read it. I can't fucking believe it! It has the next clue to release Azazel!"

"Right! It's unreal! Damn, it must be because of the Dark Prince that we're being released. I felt his powers and he's only getting stronger. I understand why we're to join our powers to destroy him!"

"Hell, yeah, he's strong. We need to go to the red cavern to search for Azazel. It's not far from here. I'm going to talk to Shasi and see if she's settled in. I'll return to pick you up in the morning."

"Right."

Samyaza nods and looks down the hall. He frowns and looks at Lyon.

"I need more time. How about the next day Lyon. I need time to talk to her. She's been sleeping and I'm not sure how she's going to feel."

Lyon nods and smiles. "Yeah, I understand. I'll come get you."

"Right."

Samyaza smiles at him and Lyon walks out of the apartment complex.

Samyaza paces around the room, running his hands through his hair. He shakes his head and looks at the sunrays on the carpet. He walks over to Crystal and watches her sleep.

She's been sleeping for so long. I'm glad that she calmed down after a while when she realized that she's home with me. Hell, she's sleeping in the bed naked. Such fucking torture. Damn, I'm still being tortured one way or another.

He leans down and moves her hair to the side and traces the curve of her face.

"Crystal, please wake up."

Crystal sighs and moves her head. She snuggles into the mattress and pillow.

"Right."

He nods and takes off his clothes. He slides into the bed with her and pulls her into his arms. He grins and closes his eyes.

Yes, now this is heaven. I'm going to sleep with her. We can talk later.

Time passes and Crystal opens her eyes. She sits up anxiously and looks around wide-eyed.

Samyaza wakes and sits up, reaching for her. "Sweetness, it's okay. I'm here. It's over and I'm not going to allow anyone to hurt you."

"Oh gawd!"

Crystal turns into him and hugs him tight, shaking and crying. "Omg Yazy, it was awful waking up naked on that altar. What was it all about? It was so freaky and totally surreal."

Samyaza holds her close and rocks her to calm her down. He moves his hand up to push her hair back.

"Sweetness, it's going to be ok. I promise."

Crystal cries and pulls back, breathing and hiccupping at the same time. Her face is covered in tears. She blinks rapidly and smiles a small smile.

Samyaza reaches for her and pulls her into his arms to kiss her. He leans back. He gazes into her passionately.

Crystal blinks rapidly to control the tears still threatening to fall. She smiles a small wavering smile.

"Thank you for rescuing me. I can't believe that the Senator is such a crazy dark person. I really did admire him but now I'm going to stay away from him."

"That's a great idea, Sweetness, because he's not what he appears. He's the Dark Prince and he's out to cause harm to humanity. He's gaining power by the second. We need to unite our powers to destroy him."

"That's why we're on a mission to locate and release the fallen angels. I need to help Lyon locate several lost Angels. He found the lead to Azazel's location. It's going to take a few days to locate him. I want to tell you the importance of our mission but also how important you are to me."

He moves his hand and cups her cheek, rubbing his thumb over her soft full lip.

"Yazy, you're so amazing and I'm so happy to meet you. I can't believe that I'm going to meet the Watchers. I thought you were all a myth."

Crystal's huge hazel eyes shine and she smiles up at him as she continues to hold him tight.

"Sweetness, you brighten my life and nurture my soul."

"I'm happy that you like me, Yazy, because I really like you."

Samyaza shakes his head, frowning. He holds her close to his heart, gazing into her eyes, searching for her feelings.

"Sweetness, you need to understand that I'm serious about you. I don't only like you but I love you and need you forever."

Crystal eyes widen. She bites her lower lip to control her elation.

"Are you serious?" She moves her hands up to push back her hair from her flushed face.

Samyaza frowns. He moves his hand up to her face to cup her right cheek. He rubs his thumb over her soft skin, enjoying the texture.

"Yes, I am serious. You're my mate and I don't plan on ever letting you go."

"Wow!"

She smiles up at him. She moves her hands up his wide shoulders, and laughs.

"Yes, wow.'

"Yazy, I'm so happy. I'm so amazed on how you quickly adjusted to everything. I mean, geeze, this is completely a different world for you."

Samyaza nods and hugs her close, burying his face in her neck.

"Crystal, the only thing that I'm thankful for is you. Nothing else is important because you're my world."

Crystal trembles, closing her eyes, and moves her face against his chest to hide her sobs.

Omg, he's amazing and I don't know how I got so lucky. I can't believe how close I feel to him, how our hearts beat as one, and how I feel all his emotions.

She pulls back and holds onto his shoulders. She gazes deeply into his beautiful violet eyes, sinking deep into his soul and merging her soul with his. She smiles softly and sexy.

"I love you, Samyaza!"

"I love you, Crystal!"

Author
P.T. Macias

I've been reading in the romance and suspense genre since I was a young girl. I dreamed of writing paranormal tales that are packed with fiery romance, incredible sexy wild men, exciting realms, and a dash of suspense.

My greatest thrill in writing the paranormal genre are the limitless range of characteristics, powers, and weaknesses available to develop the characters' and realms. I love sexy angels, gods, vampires, werewolves, dragons, and other entities.

Born and raised in San Jose, California. I now live in Sacramento, California with my gorgeous, loving husband and children. My four beautiful grandchildren are my stars. When I'm not writing I love going on cruises, to concerts, munching on white peaches, pistachio ice cream, and sipping margaritas.

Hold him close, hold him tight, and never let him go!

Leaves You Wanting More!

Multi-Genre

Paranormal Romance Fantasy Suspense

Series

De La Cruz Saga

Razer 8

Tequila 10

Secret Sexy Passions

Alpha Shifters Love

Romancing Shifters Paranormal Fantasy

The Watchers

Wolf Dynasty

Dragon Blood Legacy

Vhampiers Realm

Links

Subscribe to P.T. Macias newsletter for the latest new releases. Enjoy exclusive flash fiction, stay informed, win great prizes, and enjoy special excerpts.

Newsletter

http://www.myptmaciasbook.club/

http://ymlp.com/xghwbwqygmgj

Love me, Stalk me, and Pimp me!

https://www.facebook.com/P.T.MaciasAuthorPage/

http://www.tsu.co/

https://twitter.com/pt_macias

https://twitter.com/auth_PTMacias

http://www.amazon.com/-/e/B008B0EYWQ

Angels Of The Fallen: Azazel

The Watchers

Synopsis

The fallen angel, Azazel, has endured thousands of years in dark, isolated confinement. Finally, he's given the one chance to redeem his freedom.

Cryssi is desperate for help and runs to her twin, Crystal. She runs from her demons but finds her saving angel.

Time is running out. Evil forces threaten the very survival of the human race. Our only hope…..The Watchers.

The fate of humanity lies in the hands of these twelve stunningly sexy, sinful fallen angels.

Only destiny knows if they will save us or doom to hell.

The Watchers are waiting, wanting…needing you. It's time to live life on the dark side.

http://www.amazon.com/dp/B017J551VG

Angels Of The Fallen: Ramiel

The Watchers

Synopsis

Ramiel ceaselessly fights his demons in the dark captivity and toils on his penance. His tormented soul yearns for his beloved and her memories provide the solace and strength to endure. Time wears him down, his tired old soul is battered, and his constant light of hope is now flickering out. The Pure Blood fairy hides from her demons and fights to remain whole. The Angel of light and hope veils her. He guides her through the dark evil shadows that threaten to cloak her.

https://www.amazon.com/dp/B01CUMUUOG

Wolff's Mate

The Wolff's Essence Is For Eternity

Wolff Dynasty

The FBI Director seeks intel and discovers more than he counted on. His mate is in trouble and time is running out.

The mature widow is oblivious to what she has in her hands. The tall handsome stranger awakens her passions and love. She's forced to make life changing decisions, forget her insecurities, and liberate her passions.

Excerpt

Irene is dazed, unaware of Mayor Owens' approach or of Ice standing close by. She stares out into the ocean buried in her memories.

Mayor Owens draws near her and stops next to her. "Irene, I'm here to offer you my support." He nods and takes a seat next to her

Irene, startled, looks over at him and moves away from him. She scoots down the bench a little. She takes her hair in her hands and pulls it back, straightening her back.

"Hi Mayor Owens, that's very kind of you but I'm sure I'll be able to handle my affairs on my own." She nods and looks at him a little wary.

I've always felt an intense evil feeling when he is near. Yeah, he was close to Rex and that means he must be the same. Hell I wouldn't doubt it.

"Irene I only want to provide you some comfort and support," replies Mayor Owens, scooting closer. "I don't want you to suffer any more than you need to. I'm furious at Bryant's behavior and how he hurt you."

Irene glances over at him, she bites the inside of her mouth to control the scream that's building up deep inside her soul. I can't stand you. She closes her eyes and turns her face slightly to the right. I can't allow him to see my true feelings.

He reaches for her hand and takes advantage of her closed eyes. He brings her hand up to his lips to kiss it.

Irene is disconcerted and opens her huge sapphire eyes as soon as she feels his grasp. She quickly removes her hand out of his. She stands up urgently and turns away from him. She moves a lock of hair behind her ear with shaking hands.

"I don't need your help nor your support, and I don't want you in my life." She trembles from the intense revolution and fear she feels for him. Her face is white, her normally soft pink complexion is now completely gone, and her lower lip trembles. She shivers, she wraps her arms around herself for some warmth. I should've brought my sweater but the day looks warm and inviting.

Ice angrily grips the tree as he observes them. That asshole is stressing her out. It looks like she doesn't want him near her. What is he thinking? Who the hell is he?

Mayor Owens stands, walks to her. He reaches out with his right hand to touch her arm. "Irene allow me to help you deal with your loss."

Irene turns quickly, she pulls her arm away from his hand. She glares at him with anger. "I don't want to be a bitch but I have no choice. I'm not interested in your help, I don't want you near me, I don't want your support, and I don't want you."

She pushes her hair back, angrily. She continues to glare at Mayor Owens.

"Irene I've always found you attractive and I want to get to know you better," replies Mayor Owens, taking a step towards her.

"You're really something else. You're married and what are you offering me? You want me to be your current plaything. I'm not cut out for that." Irene shakes and glares at him angrily.

"Irene we're adults and it wouldn't hurt anyone." Mayor Owens reaches out to take her hand.

Irene pulls her hand and moves away. She turns her back, and faces the ocean. I can't believe this bastard. The nerve, he's asking me to be his new mistress, yeah right. I always felt his dark desires when he looked at me. He always made me feel dirty.

Mayor Owens clenches his hand, frustrated. I have to force her to be mine. I only want a little for just a while. What's the harm and Bryant owes me. He took his life before he paid me my share of that sweet dirty little business. Nobody knows that I'm involved.

He grabs her from the waist and turns her around. He forcefully kisses her.

Irene pushes against his shoulders. OMG, he's forcing his kiss on me. I don't like his kiss or his touch. I need to get away from him.

What the fuck! That bastard is forcing himself on her. Ice clenches his jaw tight, his jaw muscles flex and he pushes away from the tree. I need to stop him.

Without further thought, Ice storms over to Irene and Mayor Owens. He pulls her out of his grasp and he glares at him. "What the fuck are you doing with my woman!" Ice yells at him furiously.

Irene glares at Mayor Owens and then looks up at Ice. She blinks several times. Omg where did he come from? His woman? Wow he's absolutely gorgeous.

"Honey are you okay?" Ice, glances down at Irene. He gives her a huge smile full warmth. His beautiful light blue eyes sparkle with amusement.

Irene blinks, smiles up at him, and nods. "Yes Love, I'm ok. Why did you get here late? I've been waiting for you." Irene smiles up at Ice.

Oh wow, he's gorgeous and totally a huge hunk. I love his soft pale blue eyes. Yeah, he reminds me of a blond Viking.

"Honey, things came up at the office, you know how it is but I'm here now and I'm not leaving." Ice nods, and he pulls her close to his side, unconsciously.

He leans down to kiss her. He slowly tastes her lips, enjoying the texture and taste before moving inside to explore. His body explodes into a burning fiery need running rapid through his veins. Hell she's my mate.

The kiss lasts about a minute but it was a minute full of insane rapture. He pulls back grinning down at her. Hell yes, she's mine, and I feel her soul seared into mine. Damn, a human mate. I don't give a damn that she's human.

"What the fuck! Irene you're having an affair and you act all innocent with me. Damn you! You had me fooled and also poor Rex," yells Mayor Owens.

"It's not any of your business." She moves closer into Ice's warmth and support. Yes, I feel like I'm coming home.

Mayor Owens glares at them, frustrated, and angry. "I need you to answer one question. Did Rex tell you about our business?" asks Mayor Owens.

Irene blinks, and glares at him. What does he mean? Is he also part of that dirty little business? Is he afraid of being exposed? He thinks I know. Oh wow, that's a powerful card I have on him. I can keep him away from me. She nods, and smiles.

"Answer me Irene!" yells Mayor Owens. He takes a step towards her, ignoring Ice.

Beyond My Dragon's Love

Draco Celestial Realms

Synopsis

The dragon roars, fumes, and blazes! He's tired of the dragonettes' deceit. The restless Prince takes a leave from his duties and journeys to the Earth realm in search of his mate

Young, beautiful orbit engineer is forced to seduce the prince to hand over to the royal bitch, unknowingly betraying her mate. Her life takes a turn and she commits treason beyond her dragon's love.

http://www.amazon.com/dp/B013OOE5AO

Here's an excerpt

A few days later, the Hell's Night club is full of lovely young mystical beauties and Landon sits at the bar stool, watching them dance. He taps his right hand fingers on the countertop, to the beat of the blaring rock music. He turns to the right and stares into the blue eyes of a black haired werewolf.

Yeah, I've danced with her and she's lovely but no connection. He smiles at her as she sways to the music. She turns around and walks away, smiling.

A tall lovely Archaica walks towards Landon. Her hips sway softly and seductively with each graceful step, exposing a long sexy leg as the side slit parts up to her right hip. Her black fitted dress drapes softly over her curves. The sweetheart bodice pushes up her breasts, creating sexy cleavage and fullness. Her creamy breasts are showcased like pearls. The dress thin straps run up and over her shoulders, then weave down her back in a sexy pattern.

She smiles at him as she approaches the bar. She gazes into his eyes, smiling a small sexy smile. Fucking hell, yeah, I have to have a drink because I hate what I have to do. Geeze, this is unreal. Marybeth, Lisa, and Helen have tried but failed. He doesn't want to go to the hotel room. I requested time to study him and I know that he has noticed me.

Landon, nods at her. Hell, she's beautiful and I've been watching her for a few days. Oh hell, my body wants her badly.

His beautiful glowing green eyes glance down her gorgeous body. He clenches his jaw, and shifts his aching cock. He takes a drink of his whiskey, watching her approach.

Heather smiles confidently. She's on a mission. She reaches him, and slides onto the stool. She turns to Mace the bartender. "I would like a Whiskey."

Landon inhales deeply, exploding into blazing hunger. Fucking hell, her scent is simply intoxicating. Hell, she seizing my soul, and branding my blood. I feel her, I'm connecting and she's knows it. Fucking hell, I'm so ready for her. I can't fucking believe it! She's my mate! She's an Archaica! Well, she's similar to a human.

Yeah, he's a dragon, I can smell his amazing scent. Hell, he smells delicious. She closes her eyes and inhales his scent, shuddering. Hell, a delicious blazing surge flows all over my body.

Heather pushes her black hair over her shoulder with a shaky hand. What the hell does this mean? This is incredible and unreal. I need to drink this Whiskey because my body is on fire.

She takes a drink enjoying the burn as it flows down her throat, merging with her boiling blood. Hell, I'm so hot and my body is ready for him. I need him. I know it.

Landon turns towards her and he leans in close. He gazes into her beautiful huge violet eyes. I can't believe it! She has incredible violet eyes.

He continues to gaze into her eyes gauging her feelings. "I know you feel it because I can feel your heart beat. I can smell your sweet intoxicating scent, and I know you're ready for me." He looks down at her sweet red heart-shaped lips.

Heather eyes open wider, startled. Her long black eye lashes spread over her eyebrows. "You don't waste any time do you?" She bites her lower lip to control her amusement.

He looks up to gaze into her eyes, falling into her soul. "Honey, do I need to? You know it, you feel it, and your sweet pussy wants me. You're my mate and I'm not going to fight it." He leans a little closer to inhale her intoxicating, spicy arousal. Hell, my cock is going to explode. He closes his eyes and clenches his jaw.

She watches him clench his jaw, controlling his emotions. "Well, hell, tell me your name."

He opens his glowing emerald green eyes, he nods at her. "Landon Dracostar. My beautiful mate, what's your name?" He slowly takes her left hand in his. He rubs his thumb over the pulsing veins on her wrists. He closes his eyes, nodding, exuding his emerald green smoke with his bonding scent.

Heather shakes, takes a deep breath and closes her eyes. Oh hell, what should I do? Everything he said is so incredible and true. This is fucking unexpected. And what the hell. He's my mate, and I'm supposed to hand him over? Hell no! What can I do? She urgently takes another swallow of her drink, finishing it off. She turns to the bartender for more.

Landon leans in closer to her, his face a few inches away from her left cheek. His hot breath causes a sweet shiver throughout her body. "Honey, your name. Please don't torment me."

She turns her head slightly to gaze into Landon's glowing emerald-green eyes. Fucking wow. He's gorgeous, absolutely gorgeous. I never believed in mates but hell now I do. This is incredible! "Heather Mach."

He nods, leans in closer, and whispers in her ear. "My hot mate, I love your name. I want to dance with you and hold you close."

Heather shudders and nods, closing her eyes. Hell, I can't walk away from him even if I want to. There're two fucking titanic reasons forcing me to continue. He's my mate and that damn General is watching me. I feel like a traitor for what I'm going to do. Yeah, I'm going to betray my mate. Hell, fucking hell, this hurts.

"Let's dance, please." Landon whispers in her ear. He inhales her delicious scent, shuddering. He pulls her hand, slides off the stool, and turns to gaze into her tormented, confused eyes. "Honey, it's ok. You're my mate."

Heather blinks her yes, rapidly, to stop the tears then nods. What in sweet deity am I going to do? If I refuse they won't only imprison me but also get someone else to seduce him. I'm going crazy here.

She slides off the stool and follows him onto the dance floor. She walks into his arms, sighing. Oh hell, this is simply heaven. She trembles as he pulls her closer to him.

This is incredible, fucking incredible. I'm going to take her home in a few flashes. I can't wait much longer. He leans in to rest his head next to hers. He closes his eyes, and turns his head to rest his lips against her neck.

Heather slides her arms up his shoulders to his neck. She wraps her arms around his neck to pull him closer. They sway in sync to the music. For a few moments, they enjoy the new experience and knowledge of being mates.

"Landon, what are you doing here on the earth realm?" She whispers into his ear. She buries her face at the base of his neck, inhaling his delicious scent and trembles.

Hell, what can I say? That I was sick of fucking around and I was desperate to meet my mate. "Honey, honestly, I'm taking a break from my duties. What about you? Aren't you far from home? Are you working on a mission?"

Heather closes her eyes as she gasps for air, desperate to remain confident and casual. Her heart beat increases, the pulsating vein on her neck evidence of her distress.

Fucking hell, she's totally out of control. I can feel her erratic heartbeat at the vein against my lips.

"Landon, yes. I'm on a mission. I'm the Gliderspike Flash obit engineer." She inhales his scent, shuddering. Fucking wow, I'm so stoked with his scent. I so wish that we were meeting under different circumstances. Fucking wow! My heart feels heavy. It's agonizing to think of what I have to do, and I'm consumed by guilt. She closes her eyes tight to stop the tears.

Landon moves his lips near her left ear. "Honey, it's ok. There isn't anything to worry about. We're mates and I'm not going to let you go. Heather, you're my eternal mate." He releases his bonding scent with his emerald green smoke, surrounding her.

Heather turns her face into his neck, inhaling his bonding scent. I love his scent.

"I want to kiss you." He holds her closer. I know she can feel my throbbing cock.

She nods, moves her head slightly to allow him access to her lips. She moans into his mouth when he takes a deep searching kiss.

Hell yes, fucking yes. She completes me, my soul. And my dragon is ecstatic. This is what I've been searching for.

He devours her mouth, releasing his bonding scent with his emerald green smoke. His tongue sucks hers and explores every little crevice.

Amazing, simply amazing. Hell, his scent is drugging me. I can feel his hot cock burning against my pussy. Hell, yes I want him. Heather pulls back, a little dazed, and gazes into his beautiful passionate, glowing emerald-green eyes.

"Not here." She whispers, searching his eyes. "Take me home."

Landon clenches his jaw, nods. "Honey, let's walk outside." Fucking hell, I have to make sure that my aura disappears instantly. I don't want anyone tracking me home. I don't like this feeling I have. I trust her but something is off. My gut feeling is never off.

She closes her eyes, nods. Yeah, I know that it will be difficult for the General and his warriors to track. I'm going to make it difficult for the General to catch my mate. I'm don't know what they want him for.

He takes her hand and laces their fingers, then pulls her close to his side. They walk across the room weaving around the dance floor, out into the hallway, and out into the dense mist.

He stops outside the door and smiles down at her. "Honey, I'm not letting you go." He leans down to kiss her as he holds her tight. Hell, yeah. Our auras will merge into one, making it difficult to track.

He continues to kiss her deeply and holds her tight as he teleports to several different areas around the vicinity of Hell's Night club. He teleports around the city, and finally he teleports into his room.

Fucking yes. She's here in my room and soon will be in my bed. My mate is finally in my arms.

A Vhampier's Forbidden Wolf

Wolff Dynasty

Synopsis

A spoiled, sexy and wild young wolf loves the chase. She loves to stir it up and watch the fireworks. She comes to a complete stop when she meets a vhampier that rocks her world.

The mature Vhampier, the royal assassin, falls under her spell. He goes against the supernatural council, family, and royal decree.

The unexpected threat to their lives bring them together, exposing their love.

http://www.amazon.com/dp/B00WBWBU4A

Excerpt

You need to meet Prince Viktor Bach Vlastimir, aka Demise. He's the royal assassin.

Enjoy a shifters bite!

"I see that you are hungry. Cyn, tell me about you. What do you do? What are your dreams?"

Cynthia winks, and slowly chews her steak. When she's done, she grins at him, and leans in close to him.

"My dream is to fuck you silly."

He grins at her and leans in close to her ear. He whispers and nibbles her ear.

"Yeah, that's my dream too. What other dreams do you have?"

Hell, she's driving me insane. She's full of life, sexy as hell, and has taken my soul.

"I dream of …….hmmm. Well, I would love to be part of the World's Enforcers."

She bites her lower lip, smiles a sexy mischievous smile.

"I dream of meeting my mate someday and having my cubs. Viktor, I mean that I see it like this. I'm young, I have a lot of years to live. Why can't I have fun, and enjoy my life until I meet my mate? I can always have a career later, maybe after my cubs are grown. The world realms culture could mature, maybe the technology, and culture would make it easier to reach for my dreams."

Viktor narrows his eyes to hide his anger. Fuck no! Her mate? What the fuck! Why am I dying with the thought of her mating? I'm not her mate or a wolf. I can't offer her pups. I can fuck her silly but would that be enough? Will I be satisfied?

"Viktor? Did I make you mad? I hope not because my family is already mad at me. They feel that I'm too wild and spoiled because I don't want to go to school."

Viktor closes his eyes to hide his fear and anger. What the fuck should I say?

He opens his beautiful green eyes, the gold specks sparkle.

"I'm not mad."

"I hope not because I want you. I want to enjoy our time as long as it is."

Viktor smiles at her and raises her hand up to his lips. He kisses her hand and slowly turns it over to inhale her spicy rose blood. He places his lips at the veins, enjoying the rapid fiery flow of her blood.

Cynthia watches him. She shudders with wild hot hunger, and leans closer. She whispers into his ear.

"Viktor, I don't see why we should fight this wild hunger. We wouldn't hurt anyone."

She licks her lower lip, watching his lips place a hot kiss on the veins on her wrist. She trembles as a burning shiver races through her body. Her breasts swell and her nipples get harder.

Fucking hell, his lips feel so hot. I can feel his soul, and his vanilla spicy scent bleed into every pore in my body. I'm on fire and aching. What the hell! I'm not supposed to feel like this for a vhampier. I'm positive that these are feelings that I'm supposed to feel for my mate.

He looks at her breasts and nipples. He groans and looks up into her glowing blue eyes.

What the fuck, she has me totally under her spell, my body is in sync with hers, and I'm going to explode. I can feel her wild hunger, her soul is burning into mine, and I can feel her wolf.

"No, we wouldn't, but because you're young I would like to know that you're aware of the chaos that our relationship would cause."

Sugar's Fate
Wolff Dynasty

Synopsis

New in town and new at the clinic, the sexy alpha shifter has the young women in town fawning over him. He's always enjoyed sexy petite woman until he examines a BBW. The strong, unexpected mating attraction baffles and intrigues him. The delectable thought of mating crosses his mind for the first time.

Young, confident and beautiful BBW accepts her curves until she gets hurt. The unexpected feelings that she encounters when she meets the doctor confuse her. Can she overcome her doubts, accept his invitation for a date, and win his love?

Her boss sends her on a special assignment which places her in danger and risks her life. The Dr. is forced to make hard decision to save her.

http://www.amazon.com/dp/B00RY8OLZQ

Enjoy a nibble!

Artemis turns to slide onto the bed and waits for the Doctor to show. She clasps her hands tightly, closes her eyes, and nods. "Yes, I have to ask him to run some tests."

Dr. McKenzie walks down the hall to the last room. He knocks on the door, waiting for admittance.

"Come in."

He opens the door and walks into the small room. The overpowering sensual spicy scent knocks him off balance. His wolf glows brightly, burning, and flashing red. He shudders, grinds his jaw tight to control the growl that threatens to escape, and turns quickly to look at Artemis. His golden brown eyes glow. Fucking hell, she's my mate! She's the one in my dreams and fuck, she's sexy as hell. Now I'm totally out of control.

Artemis looks at him. Her eyes looks at his shiny black leather shoes, then move up his expensive, perfectly pressed navy blue wool slacks, and his white shirt under the white doctor coat. She inhales deeply, and her body explodes into a burning shiver. She shudders, her eyes moves up to his sexy jawline, and stops at his full luscious red lips. She trembles, her eyes widen. Shit, he looks and smells delicious. How embarrassing is this? The doctor is the sexist guy ever!

He smiles, slowly gazing into her beautiful green eyes. He closes the door gradually, as if in a trance, looking her over slowly, and nods. "Hello, I'm Dr.

McKenzie." He walks over to her, clenching his jaw to control his emotions.

She blushes, nods at him, moving her hands up to push her hair back from her flushed face. "Hi Dr. McKenzie." She moves her hands back to her lap and clenches them tightly together in an effort to control her emotions. A burning shiver runs through her body, the intense feelings run rampant, setting her on fire. Her nipples are sensitive and aching, protruding under the gown, so ready for his attention.

Easton's eyes narrow. They moves down the gown to her breasts, and he swallows his growl. Fucking hell, I'm dying. This is excruciatingly painful. Hell, my mate's nipples are mouthwatering, even more than in my dreams. I wonder if they're as beautiful.

He moves his gaze up, he looks into her amazing eyes searching for her recognition. She's the one in my dreams, my mate. I know it like I know that I'm going to claim her, soon. The sooner the better because I can't control my wolf for long.

He stops in front of her and inhales deeply, closing his eyes. Hell, I have to act like a professional. I don't smell a lot of wolf but she's my mate. She's only half wolf, damn it. Yeah, in my dreams that's been a factor that I haven't wanted to accept as true. She's doesn't know that she's my mate, a wolf, or else she would be all over me. Just my fucking luck. Her scent is causing chaos to my body and my cock is anxious to bury deep inside her sweet fiery pussy. I'm totally ready to fuck until we get our fill of each other because she's been teasing me and my wolf for a long time.

Artemis bites her lower lip to prevent her moan. Shit, I'm so turned on by Dr. McKenzie, like I've never been turned on by any man before. This is painful and, embarrassing, and he's totally out of my league.

She closes her eyes, the images of the man in her dreams instantly surface. She blushes and inhales, then shudders as his scent arouses her senses.

Shit, oh shit! He's the guy in my dreams. But I don't know him. How in the world could this be? Does he know me? No, no I'm crazy, he can't know me because it's only in my dreams that I see him. He doesn't have a clue who I am.

Dr. McKenzie grinds his molars, clenches his fists, and walks over to the sink. He washes his hands. I really want to throw cold water on my face to see if I can cool down this fucking need. Hell! This isn't the right place to meet your mate for the first time and especially to perform a medical evaluation when I only want to love her, but cannot. I can learn all about her later.

He turns around, forces a small smile on his lips, his feverish eyes glow. I hope that I'm not scaring her because in my dreams she's always scared of what and who I am.

"Ms. Evans, is there a particular concern that you have?" He walks slowly over to her, trying to gaze into her eyes to stay grounded.

Artemis nods, blushing. "Yes, Dr. McKenzie I would like a prescription for birth control and I would like to have some tests run."

His eyes open wide, almost a glare. Fucking hell! She wants birth control. What the fuck for? Yeah, hell not going to happen because she's mine.
He nods and turns to grab some gloves furiously out of the box on the wall. Fucking hell! I don't want to even think about that! What the fuck!

He turns around and pulls out the table's extension. "Ms. Evans, please lay back and put your heels on the stirrups. I need to examine you."

Artemis blushes, nods, and lays slowly back, closing her eyes. Oh shit, this is totally embarrassing. He's going to see my thighs and my pussy. The first man to ever see my pussy.

Easton angrily gets the speculum, he carefully slides it inside to hold the walls of the vagina apart for a clear view of the vagina. He grabs the swab to take a swab of the cervix to get an example of the cells. "Please try to relax, this will take only a few minutes."

Artemis eyes are closed tight and she inhales slowly, shuddering. Hell, this is too much. I have too many different emotions exploding in my body and mind.

He turns to look inside the vagina and notices that she's still a virgin. Hell yes! Damn it, I didn't expect this. What the fucking hell does she want the birth control if she's not sexually active?

"Ms. Evans, you're still a virgin."

Artemis tightens her eyes, nodding. "Yes." Her face turns a deeper red, almost the shade of a tomato.

Easton looks over at her, he observes her deep blush and shallow breathing. Hell, she's so embarrassed.

"Why do you want birth control?"

Artemis blushes deepens a darker red. "I don't want to get pregnant and you never know."

Hell, she can't get pregnant without me! Yeah, she doesn't know this.
He gathers the sample and carefully takes out the speculum. He then pulls the gown back down slowly, trying not to look at her beautiful pussy. Yeah, I'm a doctor, don't look at her like that. Hell, but she's my mate. She looks so delicious. Hell I want to claim her, I want my mate, my wolf wants her, and I want to get her pregnant.

He walks over to the side of the bed to look down at her. He watches her beautiful breasts rise and fall with each breath. He closes his feverish golden brown eyes. He inhales deeply, burning up at her spicy scent.

Seizing Fate

Wolff Dynasty

Synopsis

The young, hot, and sexy Dr. Grant is weary, jaded and skeptical at 99 years old. He's impatient to meet his mate, start and enjoy a family, and hold his cubs.

Kymberly, a young beauty, meets him on her birthday. She likes him, she wants him, and she is full of life.

He tries to push her away. His mate, the one he's been searching for and waiting for all his life! Now, finally he meets her. She's in front of him. The problem is that he doesn't want to touch her. Of course, he feels awful because she's so young, but he can't resist her.

The unexpected happens. The threat of losing her forces him to action.

http://www.amazon.com/dp/B00V2BVD0C

Enjoy a small bite

I'm going to share a little nibble, oh yeah!

Damn it, now what? We're here alone, darn. Grant continues to gaze into her green eyes. He's unable to resist, and searches for her soul.

"Grant?" Kymberly falls deep into his gaze, connecting with his soul.

Grant nods at her and stands up. He towers over her and walks the few steps to stop in front of her, a couple of inches between them. "Yeah?" He shoves his hands into his jeans. I need to control the wild impulse to grab her, pull her close, and kiss her. I have to resist this pull.

"I'm really happy to meet you on my twenty-first birthday because I'm glad that you're going to celebrate it with me." She moves her right hand to push her hair over her shoulder, the silver bangles jingling softly.

The movement causes her right breast to move up, drawing his attention to her sweet nipple. Grant swallows hard and takes a step back. "It's my pleasure, Kymberly."

Kymberly watches him move back and she raises an eyebrow. "Don't run from me, Grant. I know you feel it and it feels so right."

He gazes into her huge green eyes and nods. "Yeah, but I can't because you're too young." He clenches his jaw, closes his eyes, and shudders as her scent seeps into his body and soul.

He releases his bonding scent, his wolf ready to claim his mate, and not willing to wait. He inhales deeply and a deep growl starts to rumble deep in his chest, ready to flow out. He clenches his jaw tight to keep it in.

"Hmm….you smell delicious." She closes her eyes, smiles a sexy small smile, and nods. She licks her lower lip and opens her eyes to gaze into his surprised eyes.

"You smell my scent?" Hell, that's incredible. Damn it.

"Yes, you smell like spice, sandalwood, and incredible." She nods, closing her eyes and inhaling deeply.

His body releases more of his bonding scent and he trembles. No, no I need to control this because I can't scare her off. Hell, I'm not sure how to deal with her, a human mate? Damn it.

She opens her eyes and searches his eyes for his thoughts. "You're going to spend the evening with me, right?" I don't know why I feel that he wants to run. I know that he feels this connection.

Grant nods and smiles a small smile. "Yes."

"Promise?"

"Yes, I promise."

Free Books
Loco, Razer 8
Razer 8

Razer 8 takes you into the world of organized crime, kidnapping, politics, military romance and suspense thriller. Razer 8 Delta Force operatives are full of passion. Enjoy these amazing passionate men, a thrilling ride, and a dash of love!

The hard driven, ambitious delta force elite operative is immune to women. His heart has been destroyed by a treacherous woman and the unexpected loss of his family. These events have driven him nearly into insanity. The hard knocks in life propel him into grasping his emotions, his thoughts, and his physical condition. He focused on his goal. Loco doesn't allow any type of distractions or obstacles to stop him. His actions and recklessness have earned him his nickname, Loco.

The Infinite power, Razer 8 operatives, are united and linked for infinity. His team mates recognize his pain, anger, and strength is derived from the intense impotency he feels from his loss.

The unexpected mission and unexpected encounter with his soul mate, tests his strength. His mind, heart, and soul recognize his love even before the actual encounter. The ruthless criminals threaten to harm his soul mate, pushing and transforming him into a fearless warrior.

http://www.amazon.com/dp/B00EUTD482

P.T. Macias Books
Wicked Blush, Supernatural Realm Enforcers Elite Ops

Tequila 10

Synopsis

Wicked Blush, a beautiful dragonette, is sad and frustrated. She refuses to return to her realm to marry the stranger that she was promised to at the time of her birth. Blush has reached the fork in the road and now she has to make some soul wrenching decisions.

A handsome stranger at the Christmas party draws her in and she chooses to forget her fiancé. This Christmas, there's a special gift for more than one of the elite operatives.

Her decision takes her on an incredible journey of secrets, deep passions, and truths. Will she be able to keep her heart? Can she escape her destiny and her soul mate?

Blush is one of ten special operatives that work with the government, using their special abilities but also have their own agenda. These special operative's monitor the supernatural community, even as they're swept into a whirlwind of love, truths, and untold passions. The supernatural realms are threatened and endangered. Time is running out! The enforcers are desperate to stop the menace.

http://www.amazon.com/dp/B00OYXMQMY

Small nibble

Connor leans against the wall next to the window watching Josephine aka Blush.

Blush stops in front of the huge Christmas tree. She looks for Storm or Cassie. Geeze, I just saw them, where did they go?

Blush is wearing a beautiful silky shimmering dusty rose dress that shimmers when she moves. The sweetheart bodice is fitted down to the waist, the dress has straps that fall off her shoulder in a cascade of material, and the skirt is a beautiful sheer chiffon that flares out in a cloud around her thighs. She's wearing incredible silver strappy shoes that sparkle.

She moves her head and the beautiful diamond chandelier drop earrings sparkle as she moves. Blush moves her right hand up to her waist and looks around the room. The beautiful diamond bracelet that looks like a wide cuff sparkles brilliantly.

Connor takes a drink of his coke. Ah, I love her beautiful sapphire blue eyes. Hell yes, she's wearing the diamond cuff bracelet that I sent her for her birthday. I wonder if she's aware of this.

Geeze, almost everyone is a couple. Only a few of us on the team are still single. Hmm, it's not like I can fall for someone when I'm already engaged. Yeah, to someone I don't' know. This sucks. She moves her hand to adjust a strand of hair that escaped her diamond clip.

Hmmm, I can feel someone watching me. Who could it be? Wow, I know everyone here. She slowly turns to look around and notices the handsome young man leaning against the wall near the window. *Uh, I don't know him but I can tell that he's a dragon.*

She looks at him glancing down to his black shiny leather shoes. She then moves her gaze up his black slacks, up to perfectly fitted black classic tuxedo. She narrows her eyes, nodding her pleasure. *Oh yeah, the tux fits him perfectly.*

Oh yeah, my dragonette is a beauty. I love her style and her black hair is silky shiny beautiful. Connor takes a drink of his coke.

Blush gaze moves up to scrutinize his perfect square jawline that has a short black goatee framing his luscious full red lips. She bites her lower lip, moving her gaze up to his eyes.

He moves his gaze up to her beautiful face and gazes right into her beautiful eyes.

Hell yes, she's noticing me. She doesn't have a clue she's mine. I love her blue sapphire eyes.

Omg, those eyes are truly clear turquoise, my favorite color. I've only met a few people that have that beautiful shade of clear turquoise that sparkles.

Blush gazes into his eyes falling, falling deep into his soul. She blinks rapidly, she's shaken, and blushing. She turns around and walks over to Storm and Dawn walking into the hall with the babies in their arms.

Omg, omg I felt his soul and I swear mine merged with his. I can't do that. I'm engaged and I can't fall in love with someone here on earth even if he's a dragon.

Connor pushes away from the wall and shoves his hands into his pockets. *Oh Hell yes, she recognizes that she's my soul mate. She felt our souls merge. I want to run after her so badly but I can't. I know that she's afraid of her feelings.*

He turns to walk over to the bar to get another coke. *Oh hell, I need another drink.*

Becoming Her Master

An Incredible Journey Of
Love, Surrender, and Passions
Secret Sexy Passions

Synopsis

Beautiful, ambitious, gritty Eva loves David Adrian but has other plans for her future. Despite the fact that they've been together for a while, she coquettishly evades committing to him.

David Adrian adores Eva but she has other plans. Eva evades making a commitment and he's feed up so he gives her an ultimatum.

Eva and David Adrian are in love and they have a great chemistry. David Adrian realizes that Eva enjoys a little dominance, bondage, and submission. Their relation evolves and he becomes her Master.

An Incredible Journey Of Love, Surrender, and Passions.

http://www.amazon.com/dp/B00M5EVJA4

Made in the USA
San Bernardino, CA
09 June 2016